SPECIAL MESSAGE TO READERS

THE THIRD KEY

The Reverend Colin Armitage receives a parcel one morning containing a key and the intriguing message: 'This is Bluebeard's first key.' The key belongs to the cottage of a woman named Sylvia Shand, who is found there, strangled. A few days later, Bluebeard's second key arrives by post and the district nurse is found strangled in similar circumstances. The police believe a homicidal maniac is loose in the village but Armitage has other ideas. And then a third key arrives . . .

GERALD VERNER

THE THIRD KEY

Complete and Unabridged

LINFORD
Leicester

First published in Great Britain

First Linford Edition
published 2014

A catalogue record for this book is available
from the British Library.

ISBN 978–1–4448–1871–0

Published by
F. A. Thorpe (Publishing)
Anstey, Leicestershire

Set by Words & Graphics Ltd.
Anstey, Leicestershire
Printed and bound in Great Britain by
T. J. International Ltd., Padstow, Cornwall

This book is printed on acid-free paper

For Christopher with love

1

Mrs. Armitage looked across the break-fast table at her daughter and sighed. Her pleasant face wore an expression of half-humorous irritability.

'It really *is* too bad of your father, Merle,' she said. 'The coffee's cold and his bacon will be quite spoiled keeping hot in the oven. All scrumped up and brittly — so nasty and not a bit nourish-ing . . . ' She broke off as the door of the sunny breakfast-room opened, but it was only a thin and rather untidy-looking girl who thrust in her head and said, nasally:

'D'yer want some more 'ot water?'

'I think you'll have to make a fresh pot of coffee,' said Mrs. Armitage. 'Did you tell the vicar that breakfast was ready, Linda?'

'I've told 'im twice,' answered Linda. 'He doesn't take no notice.'

'Well, be a good girl and tell him again,' said Mrs. Armitage. 'Perhaps he didn't hear you before.'

The untidy girl nodded, removed her head, and the door shut with a bang.

'You ought to know what Daddy's like by now,' remarked Merle, putting a large portion of marmalade on a microscopic piece of toast. 'It's always the same when he's in the middle of a new book. He's probably under the impression that he's *had* his breakfast.'

'I know, dear, I know,' said her mother, 'but I wish he *would* realise how very trying it is keeping meals hanging about — especially these days when it's *so* difficult to get servants . . . '

'Daddy was up very early this morning, wasn't he?' asked Merle. She asked more to sidetrack her mother from the question of the servant problem than because she was seeking information. It was one of Mrs. Armitage's pet worries and she was always prepared to launch into a long dissertation on the subject at the slightest provocation.

'At the crack of dawn, dear,' answered Mrs. Armitage. 'He was trying to be very quiet and not disturb anybody. It was like a minor earthquake!'

Merle laughed.

'Poor Daddy!' she said. 'He does write jolly good books, though, you know, and they bring in quite a lot of money. The stipend of the Reverend Colin Armitage wouldn't go very far unless it was augmented by the income of 'Armitage Crane,' the well-known writer of detective stories.'

'That's true enough, dear,' agreed Mrs. Armitage, 'although it has always seemed to me a little incongruous that a clergyman should write stories about murders . . .'

'Daddy's murders are all very highbrow, Mummy,' said Merle.

Mrs. Armitage looked a little doubtful.

'I suppose they are,' she said, 'if you can call any murder highbrow. All the same it's hardly the thing one associates with a clergyman — especially the vicar of a parish . . .'

'I don't know why not,' said Merle. 'The Bible is full of murders . . .'

'Oh, really, Merle,' said her mother in a slightly shocked tone. 'I don't think that's quite a proper thing to say.'

'It's true, isn't it?' retorted Merle obstinately. 'Look at Cain and Abel and that woman, what's-her-name, who killed thingummybob with a nail . . . Daddy pinched *that* idea for his last book, *Nail in the Head.*'

'I know,' said Mrs. Armitage, still in a slightly disapproving voice, 'but I still don't quite like the idea. There are a number of people in the village who strongly disapprove of your father's books . . . '

'Only people like Mrs. Godwyne-Sands and Miss Crimp. They disapprove of everything on principle — even sunbathing . . . '

Mrs. Armitage remembered that occasion with embarrassment.

'Well, my dear,' she said, 'that swimming suit you were wearing, when they saw you on the lawn, was just a trifle — well, *brief*. Now, wasn't it?'

'It's not much use sunbathing in a winter overcoat, is it?' said Merle reasonably.

'There was a great difference between the suit you were wearing and a winter coat,' declared Mrs. Armitage.

'It was quite respectable,' said Merle. 'They're being worn at all the best places this summer . . . '

'No doubt, but it was hardly suitable

4

for the vicarage lawn,' said Mrs. Armitage firmly.

'They're just nasty-minded old cats!' said Merle. 'If they really want someone to be disapproving about, they should start on Sylvia Shand . . . '

'They have — very definitely,' said her mother.

'I'm pretty broad-minded,' said Merle, 'but she's the limit! Those parties she gives at her cottage are . . . well, they *are*, aren't they?'

'I have no wish to hear anything about them,' said Mrs. Armitage hastily. 'I don't think it's the kind of thing that you should talk about . . . '

'Oh, don't be silly, Mummy,' interrupted Merle. 'I'm not a child. I'm twenty-two . . . '

'There are some things it is better not to discuss at any age,' declared Mrs. Armitage, who immediately proceeded to discuss them. 'I am quite prepared to admit that the woman behaves disgracefully. I am very thankful to say that she has only rented the cottage for the summer . . . '

'The Stantons should have had more sense than to let it to a woman like that,' said Merle.

'Perhaps they didn't know what she was like until it was too late,' said Mrs. Armitage. 'And talking of the Stantons, dear, did you know that Richard Stanton, Sir Robert's brother, is back?'

Merle nodded.

'Yes, I saw him yesterday in the High Street,' she said. 'I thought he looked terribly ill and rather — queer.'

Mrs. Armitage, attracted by the peculiar intonation of the word 'queer', looked at her daughter sharply.

'What do you mean by 'queer'?' she demanded.

'I don't know ... it's difficult to explain,' answered Merle, frowning. 'A sort of funny look about the eyes ... I can't really describe it ... '

'The sun, I expect,' said Mrs. Armitage. 'It's very hot in South Africa, you know.'

'He didn't look to me as if he'd been anywhere where there was much sun,' began Merle.

She broke off as the door opened and

the Reverend Colin Armitage came in. He was a thin-faced, grey-haired man with the slight stoop of the scholar. He peered genially at them through a pair of pinc-nez with the expression of a benevolent and rather absent-minded sheep.

'Good morning, my dear — good morning, Merle,' he said in a slight tone of surprise, as though it was rather unusual to see them there. 'Is — er — breakfast ready?'

He came over and sat down at the table.

'Breakfast has been ready for over an hour, Colin,' said Mrs. Armitage. 'We have been keeping your bacon hot in the oven . . . '

'Why didn't somebody tell me?' inquired the Reverend Colin Armitage mildly.

'You're incorrigible, Daddy,' said Merle, laughing. 'Linda told you three times . . . '

'Did she?' Her father looked at her in extreme surprise. 'Um, now I come to think of it I *do* have a vague recollection that she was trying to tell me something. I'm afraid I didn't pay much attention. I was in the middle of a rather tricky alibi . . . '

'I do wish you'd try and be more punctual for meals, Colin,' said Mrs. Armitage. 'It makes things so difficult. Merle, will you tell Linda . . . '

Merle got up, but there was no need to tell the untidy Linda, for she appeared at that moment with a plate on which reposed an unpleasant-looking collection of curled-up black strips which might have been anything but certainly had no resemblance to bacon. This she deposited with a thump on the table in front of the Reverend Colin Armitage.

'Oh, dear,' said Mrs. Armitage, peering at this unappetising dish. 'I think you had better do some fresh . . . '

'No, no,' said her husband. 'This will do admirably, Mary, admirably. I prefer my bacon — er — well done . . . '

'You've got it,' said Merle. 'It's like tinder . . . '

'I'll fetch the coffee,' said Linda and went out.

'At least the coffee will be fresh,' said Mrs. Armitage. 'Are you quite sure that you wouldn't like some fresh bacon, Colin? That really looks quite uneatable . . . '

'No, no. This is excellent — excellent,' declared the Reverend Colin Armitage, making no attempt to eat it, but fiddling with the cruet. 'Dear me, you know, it's entirely a question of the clock . . .'

Merle made a grimace at her mother.

'It's quite hopeless,' she said.

'Will you have your breakfast, Colin, please,' said Mrs. Armitage.

Her husband looked at her with a completely blank expression.

'Breakfast, my dear?' he said vaguely. 'Oh, yes — yes, indeed. It was very nice — very nice.'

Mrs. Armitage gave an exasperated twitch to her plump shoulders. She opened her mouth to comment on her husband's statement but the fresh arrival of Linda stopped her. Linda was armed with a coffee pot, an assortment of letters and a small parcel. She banged the coffee pot down in front of Mrs. Armitage, and thrust the letters and the parcel under the vicar's nose.

'Post's just been,' she announced unnecessarily, and departed with a rush, letting the door slam behind her.

'I do wish that girl would learn not to bang doors,' said Mrs. Armitage, pouring out coffee. 'She seems to find it quite impossible to enter or leave a room quietly . . . '

'I'll have another cup of coffee, please, Mummy,' said Merle. 'Is there anything for me, Daddy?'

'Anything . . . ? Oh, yes, I see. The post, yes.' The vicar sorted through the various envelopes. 'No, I'm afraid not, Merle . . . This appears to be a bill from Jorkins . . . I was under the impression that I had paid it . . . Um, this looks like a letter from the churchwardens. I wonder what they can be writing to *me* about? The meeting . . . '

'Drink your coffee while it's hot, Colin,' interrupted Mrs. Armitage.

'Coffee? Oh, yes — yes my dear, certainly,' said the vicar, making no effort to do so, but peering with interest at the small parcel. 'Now, I wonder what this can be?'

'Why not try opening it?' suggested Merle.

'An excellent idea, my dear,' agreed the vicar. Very carefully he proceeded to unwrap the small packet. Inside was a flat cardboard box, and inside the cardboard box lay something wrapped in tissue-paper. The Reverend Colin Armitage took it out and removed the tissue-paper covering.

It was a key.

Armitage peered at it as it lay in the palm of his hand, with a puzzled frown.

'Extraordinary,' he remarked. 'Why should anyone want to send me an old key?'

Merle got up and, coming round behind him, looked over his shoulder.

'Isn't there a note or anything with it?' she asked.

'Ah, possibly there may be,' said her father. He put the key carefully down on the table and began to search among the paper packing.

'Will you drink your coffee,' broke in the now almost despairing voice of Mrs. Armitage.

'Just a moment, just a moment, my dear,' murmured her husband. 'This is really rather intriguing . . . Yes, here we are . . .'

He extracted from the litter of the packing a small slip of paper. Smoothing it out, he stared down at it.

'Is this some kind of a joke on your part, or some of your friends, Merle?' he asked.

'A joke,' said his daugher. 'Why, what do you mean?' She leaned farther over his shoulder and looked down at the slip of paper. Now she could see that a line of writing had been roughly printed in capital letters on it. A single line of writing that read:

'THIS IS BLUEBEARD'S FIRST KEY'

'What on earth does it mean?' she asked in bewilderment. 'It's like the beginning of a detective story . . . '

'Exactly,' agreed her father, nodding. 'That's why I wondered, Merle — if, perhaps, some misplaced sense of humour . . . ?'

'I don't know anything about it, Daddy — honestly I don't,' she protested. 'I suppose it must be a joke?'

The vicar considered, still frowning at the slip of paper before him.

'I cannot think of any other explanation. Somebody has, I should imagine, tried to — er — take a rise out of me . . . '

'Who could it be?' Merle picked up the wrapping. 'Look at the postmark. It was posted in the village . . . '

Her father nodded.

'I had already noticed that, my dear. It really is most extraordinary . . . '

The expression on his daughter's face changed suddenly.

'Let me look at that key,' she said sharply.

The sudden change in her voice made Armitage look up at her in astonishment.

'Why, what's the matter, my dear?' he began mildly.

'Let me look at that key,' said Merle again. She reached down over his shoulder and picked up the key that lay beside his plate. 'I thought so,' she said after one look at it. 'Do you know what this is? This is the key to Sylvia Shand's cottage.'

'Bless my soul, is it?' exclaimed the vicar, and there was genuine surprise in his voice. 'How do you know that?'

'Because of this file cut across the handle,' answered Merle. She stabbed at it with a pointed finger nail. 'Don't you remember? It's about five years ago now. The Lazenbys had the cottage then and they went away for a holiday and left the key with us. Tommy Pritchet and I pinched it one day and went exploring. It was Tommy who filed that cut. There was an awful row about it . . . '

'Yes, yes, I remember the incident now,' said the vicar.

'But why,' interposed Mrs. Armitage, 'should the Shand woman send *you* the key to her cottage, Colin . . . ?'

'Her idea of being funny, I suppose,' said Merle indignantly.

'Well, I fail to see anything in the least amusing in it,' said Mrs. Armitage. 'Do you, Colin?'

The Reverend Colin Armitage was several seconds before he replied. Then he said, and his voice was very grave:

'No, my dear. Nothing amusing at all. I am beginning to think that it may be very serious — very serious indeed.'

2

He looked so serious, and the gravity in his voice was so pronounced, that both Merle and Mrs. Armitage stared at him in astonishment.

'What on earth do you mean?' demanded his daughter. 'How could it be serious?'

He picked up the slip of paper and scrutinised it short-sightedly.

'Do you remember what Bluebeard's wife found when she unlocked the door of the forbidden room?' he inquired gently.

'You're not suggesting . . . Oh, really, Daddy, that *is* a lot of nonsense,' cried Merle. 'You're just trying to make a plot for a detective story out of it.'

Her father looked up at her with a slightly one-sided smile curving the corners of his thin mouth.

'It would make an excellent opening for one,' he admitted, and then his face grew serious again as he pursed his lips thoughtfully. 'I don't like it,' he continued. 'I don't like it at all. I don't like the possible meaning behind that message and the key.' He shook his head. 'The more I think of it the *less* I like it.'

Mrs. Armitage sniffed.

'I think you're being quite ridiculous, Colin,' she said. 'It's somebody's stupid idea of a joke.'

'Possibly, my dear, possibly,' said the vicar, but the expression on his face remained serious. 'You may be right. I hope you are. But I intend to return this key to Miss Shand's cottage at once . . . '

'Well, please have your breakfast first,' said Mrs. Armitage. 'Linda is waiting to clear away and if she gets behind, the whole morning will be disorganised.'

'Breakfast?' answered her husband, as though he had never heard of the word. 'Oh, yes, of course, of course. I think it would be as well if I took Inspector Blane with me . . . '

'I don't know how you can be so absurd, Colin,' declared Mrs. Armitage crossly. 'That woman will only laugh at you.'

The vicar got up.

'I shall be greatly relieved if she does,' he remarked quietly. 'But I'm rather afraid she won't.'

'Daddy,' said Merle, her face suddenly white. 'What do you expect to find?'

The Reverend Colin Armitage picked up the key and slipped it into his pocket.

'That I can't tell you, my dear,' he answered. 'But I'm under the impression that it might be something rather — unpleasant.'

★　★　★

It was one of those perfect mornings in early June when the mere fact of being alive is breathtaking and wonderful. The whole earth is enchanted and there is a feeling of peace that drenches the soul and makes all the pettifogging little problems of everyday life seem remote and unreal. A haze hung over the countryside, and there was the indescribable scent of hay mingled with flowers in the air that only comes from wide, sun-heated meadows and rural gardens.

The village of Lesser Sweeping was, as yet, unspoiled by the ubiquitous builder of 'desirable residences' or the even more destructive hands of an unimaginative development corporation. It consisted of a handful of cottages, a High Street with half a dozen small shops, the church — a beautiful piece of old English architecture — and several farms. There were on the outskirts three or four large houses, built for the most part of aged, mellow brick and set in their own grounds, and of these the largest and most imposing was the Manor belonging to the Stantons. There had, as far as memory would reach, always been a Stanton at the Manor; and indeed, the family owned the greater part of the village, including the Stanton Arms, the old whitewashed pub at the foot of the High Street.

It was nine o'clock when the vicar's rather dilapidated car nosed its way down a narrow, hedge-lined lane and drew up at the gate of a small and very picturesque cottage, nestling in a garden that was gay and flaming with roses.

'Well, here we are, sir,' remarked a

18

stoutish, red-faced man, who looked more like a farmer than a policeman. 'It doesn't look to me as if anyone's up yet, do it?'

The Reverend Colin Armitage opened the door and slid out from behind the wheel. He stood for a moment staring at the cottage. There was no sign of life. The windows were all closed and the curtains still drawn. Merle and Inspector Blane joined him.

'Everything seems pretty peaceful to me, sir,' remarked the inspector. 'We seem to've come on a wild goose chase.'

'A graveyard is pretty peaceful, Blane,' said Armitage.

His daughter gave a little shiver.

'Daddy — what a horrible simile . . . '

'Come now, sir,' remonstrated the inspector. 'You've no real call for believing the lady's dead, now 'ave you? Only this key . . . '

'I dislike the implication of that message,' said the vicar. He went over to the little white painted gate and pushed it open delicately with one finger. 'Don't touch it, Merle,' he warned.

19

The inspector grinned.

'Bit early to bother about prints, sir,' he suggested. 'We don't know there's anything wrong yet . . . '

'And then it would be too late,' remarked the vicar. He held open the gate with the tip of his finger and motioned for them to enter the garden. They did so, Inspector Blane a little reluctantly.

'What are you going to do next, sir?' he asked dubiously.

'We'll knock first,' answered Armitage. He walked slowly up the narrow, flagged path to the porch. The white-painted front door was provided with a shiny black knocker and on this he beat a loud tattoo.

They waited but there was no response. Inspector Blane fidgeted uneasily. Merle felt her heart beating rather faster than normal. She hadn't believed that they would find anything wrong. She was convinced, in her own mind, that the whole thing was a joke on someone's part against her father. But it was very still and silent inside the cottage. Of course, there was always the possibility that Sylvia

Shand was away . . .

Armitage waited for a few moments and then he knocked again. Still there was no reply.

The vicar began to fumble in his pocket. After a moment he produced the key. There was a stifled exclamation from Inspector Blane.

'Here, sir,' he protested, 'you can't do that . . . '

Armitage looked at him calmly.

'Why not?' he asked.

'Well, sir, it's against the law . . . ' began the inspector in a shocked voice.

The Reverend Colin Armitage dismissed the objection with a wave of his hand. 'I have every intention of seeing what is inside this cottage,' he declared.

'Supposing the lady is in bed and asleep, sir,' said the worried Inspector Blane.

'Then,' declared Armitage, 'we can apologise and go away.'

He inserted the key in the lock and turned it.

'Look here, sir.' Inspector Blane laid a restraining hand on the vicar's arm,

'We've no right to . . . '

'I know, I know,' interrupted Armitage impatiently. 'It's contrary to regulations. I know all that, Inspector, but don't worry. I'll take full responsibility.'

He pushed against the door and it opened. At that moment they heard the sound of an approaching car coming down the lane. With the door partially open, Armitage paused and looked back towards the little gate. The car, a small black saloon, ran past the gate and suddenly pulled up with a squeal of brake-drums.

'It's Doctor Mortimer,' said Merle. 'He's seen us.'

Inspector Blane gave an unhappy grunt.

The black saloon car ran back a few paces and stopped. A red face was thrust out of the window.

'Hi there!' bellowed a thick voice. 'That you, Armitage? What the deuce are you doing . . . ?' Doctor Mortimer suddenly caught sight of Inspector Blane. 'Blane too, eh? What's happening? Anything the matter?'

'It's the vicar, here,' explained the inspector awkwardly. 'He seems to think . . . '

'Come here, Mortimer,' called Armitage. 'It may be a lucky thing that you happened to come along.'

Doctor Mortimer squeezed a ponderous bulk out of the small car and came lumbering up the path. He was a heavily-built man with a mop of unruly grey hair and a great pendulous jaw.

'What's the matter?' he demanded.

'We don't know that there's anything the matter, sir,' said Blane.

'We shall know very soon,' said the vicar. 'You may as well come in with us, Mortimer. You may be needed.'

The doctor frowned.

'Don't understand . . . ' he began.

'The vicar, here, thinks something's happened to Miss Shand,' interpolated the inspector.

'Good thing if it has,' grunted Doctor Mortimer. 'What d'you think's happened to the woman, Armitage?'

'That is what I am very curious to find out,' answered Armitage. He pushed the door fully open and stepped into the tiny hall. The others crowded in behind him, Inspector Blane bringing up the rear with a very worried expression on his face.

There was no sound from inside the cottage. The whole place was in complete and utter silence.

The Reverend Colin Armitage stood quite still at the foot of the narrow staircase, listening intently.

The hall was small and square. Two doors opened off it, one on either side, and both were shut. A narrow passage ran to the back of the premises beside the staircase, which faced the front door.

Armitage, after a slight pause, moved towards the closed door on the right of the hall and gently turned the handle. Inspector Blane swallowed hard, and the worried expression on his face deepened.

'It's your responsibility, sir, if any trouble comes of this,' he whispered hoarsely.

The vicar motioned him to silence. Opening the door he peered into the room beyond. It was very small, and furnished as a dining-room. A polished gate-legged table occupied the centre, and against one wall was an oak sideboard. In one corner stood a modern cocktail cabinet. Chairs were grouped round the centre table, and there were large bowls of flowers on the table and on the sideboard. The scent of them came wafting out to them. But the room was empty.

Armitage withdrew, closed the door quietly, and went over to the other door. Turning the handle, he opened it slowly. Merle, looking over his shoulder, saw that this room was larger than the other. It was furnished as a lounge. There was a settee, heaped with gaily coloured cushions, two easy chairs, and a television set. As in the other room there were flowers everywhere . . .

But there was something else here that had *not* been in the other room — something that caused the breath to hiss sharply through the vicar's suddenly shut teeth and made Merle clutch at his arm in terror.

In front of the television set, sprawled in an unnatural and ungainly position, like a doll that had been flung down, was the figure of a woman. A woman whose blonde hair was dishevelled and whose face . . .

'Go away, Merle,' said Armitage sternly.

'Go away. It's not a very pleasant sight . . .'

'It's horrible . . . horrible . . . ' whispered Merle, her face white and her eyes staring.

'What is it, sir?' asked Inspector Blane from behind them.

'It's Miss Shand,' answered the vicar. 'You'd better have a look at her, Mortimer . . . '

Doctor Mortimer edged his large bulk past them and peered into the room. His heavy face changed as the muscles round his jaw tightened. He thrust his way unceremoniously into the room and dropped on one knee beside that distorted figure.

'She's dead,' he announced after a quick glance.

'Bluebeard's Chamber,' muttered the Reverend Colin Armitage.

Inspector Blane, suddenly becoming the official representative of the law, pushed the vicar aside and entered the room.

'How did she die, doctor?' he asked.

Doctor Mortimer pointed to the swollen face, blue-tinged even under the heavy make-up.

'Strangulation,' he answered briefly.

'Don't touch anything, please,' said Blane authoritatively. 'It looks like murder . . . '

'Of course it's murder, man,' snapped Mortimer impatiently. 'D'you think she could have tied *that* round her own throat?'

He pointed to the thin cord which was just visible, knotted round the dead woman's neck.

3

'I've a mind,' said Superintendent Mac-Donald thoughtfully, 'that we're going to be up against a very difficult job with this case.'

'I agree with you, sir,' said Inspector Blane.

It was the afternoon of the same day on which the dead body of Sylvia Shand had been found in the lounge of the cottage she had rented for the summer, and Super-intendent MacDonald and Inspector Blane were sitting in the big, comfortably shabby study at the Vicarage.

Superintendent MacDonald, a big raw-boned Scot, with a face that looked as if it had been hewn out of a block of solid teak, had been summoned from the neighbouring town of Midchester to conduct the investigation into the wom-an's death. All the preliminary details that constitute an inquiry in a murder case had been complied with. The police photographers and fingerprint experts had completed their work at the cottage, the police surgeon had confirmed Doctor Mortimer's diagnosis of the cause of death, and the body of the murdered woman had been removed for the post mortem examination. The cottage, shut up and sealed, had been left in the charge of a police constable. Superintendent MacDonald had interviewed a number of people in the village of Lesser Sweeping, from whom he had gathered all the information he could regarding the dead woman and which, he found, was disappointingly meagre. Now, in company with Inspector Blane, he had come up to the Vicarage to see the Reverend Colin Armitage and gather such additional information as was possible.

MacDonald was a shrewd and canny Scot and he knew that under the vicar's diffident and absent-minded manner was a first-class brain, and he was not averse to gathering such crumbs of wisdom as the Reverend Colin Armitage might let fall. The reputation of 'Armitage Crane' was well-known, and MacDonald had a lurking conviction that the mind that was capable of working out the intricate plots which had been responsible for that reputation, might quite conceivably be of value in contributing to the solution of this real-life problem. He had already had sufficient proof of this in the fact that, but for the vicar's shrewdness over the key, the murder might not have been discovered for a considerable time.

'Aye,' he repeated, 'a very difficult job. From the information I've been able to gather so far, the dead woman possessed a considerable number of friends who were in the habit of visiting her at frequent intervals. They'll all have to be traced, and questioned concerning their movements at the time the murder was committed.' He looked over at Doctor Mortimer whose huge bulk occupied a large easy chair near the open window. 'According to you and the police surgeon,' MacDonald went on, 'the murder actually took place between the hours of ten o'clock and midnight.'

'That's as near as you can put it,' grunted Mortimer. 'We found the body at nine-thirty this morning and the woman had then been dead for approximately twenty-two hours . . . '

'Which would fit in with my reception of the key by the first post this morning,' remarked Armitage from behind his big, littered writing table.

Superintendent MacDonald nodded.

'Ah, yes — the key,' he said. 'I was coming round to that, sir. It's a very remarkable thing that key — a very remarkable thing.'

'I thought it extremely odd,' said the vicar.

'It was posted in the village to catch the three-thirty collection on Thursday afternoon, sir,' put in Inspector Blane.

'Aye — the postmark told us that,' said MacDonald.

'That's our last collection,' said Mortimer. He pulled out a large handkerchief and mopped his heavy face.

'If it had been posted on Wednesday night — the night of the murder — or in the early hours of Thursday morning, it would have caught the *first* collection,' said the vicar thoughtfully. 'That's at eight-thirty a.m. Now that's rather a significant point.'

'You mean that it indicates someone local, sir?' said MacDonald.

Armitage nodded slowly.

'Don't you think so?' he said. 'If it was someone outside the district it's hardly likely that he would hang about the scene of the crime until the following day.'

'Unless he stayed the night in the dead woman's cottage, sir,' said the superintendent. 'That's a possibility.'

'Surely the natural instinct would be to get away as quickly as possible,' said Mortimer.

'There could have been a very good reason for staying, doctor,' answered MacDonald. 'For instance — if the murderer came by train, he'd realise that there would be less chance of being remembered if he travelled back during the daytime, when there'd be more people about. Or again there might not have been a train available.'

'Rather a risky thing to do, don't you think?' said Mortimer.

'Less risky than you imagine,' remarked

Armitage. 'In fact he would have been safer there than anywhere . . . ' He took off his pince-nez, peered at them with a surprised expression as though wondering what on earth they could be, and put them on again. 'It's very peculiar that, you know,' he continued. 'Yes, very peculiar.'

'What is, sir?' asked MacDonald.

'Up to the beginning of the week,' said the vicar almost as though he were talking to himself, 'a very respectable woman, Mrs. Dawlish, who lives in the village, used to go up to Miss — er — Shand's cottage every morning to do the cleaning. On Monday there was some sort of trouble — about the amount of work that she was expected to do, I believe, and Mrs. Dawlish refused to go any more . . . '

MacDonald looked rather bewildered for a moment and then his face cleared.

'You mean, sir,' he said, 'that in the normal course of events, it would have been this woman who would have discovered the murder — when she went in the morning to clean?'

'Exactly,' agreed Armitage.

'So unless you'd received the key this

morning and concluded there was something wrong — very smart of you, sir, if you don't mind my saying so — the murder might not have been discovered for some time?'

'Yes,' said the vicar. 'And that's rather extraordinary, isn't it? It would seem that the murderer *wanted* his crime to be discovered as soon as possible . . . '

'But that's ridiculous,' broke in Mortimer. 'Surely, the longer it remained undiscovered the better chance he had of getting away?'

'You'd think so, wouldn't you?' remarked MacDonald. He raised a bony hand and gently scratched his chin. 'If that was the reason for sending the key he must have known about the row with Mrs. Dawlish. Umm. Pointing again to someone local, eh?'

'I am under the impression,' said the Reverend Colin Armitage, 'that the person who committed the murder is very well versed in local affairs. The choice of myself, as the recipient of the key, rather tends to bear this out.'

'I think you're right, sir,' said Inspector

Blane. 'I don't expect anyone else would have taken much notice of it. And, of course, if your daughter hadn't recognised what key it was from the cut on the handle . . . '

'Quite so,' assented Armitage. 'That, I believe, was one of the considerations that decided the murderer's choice.'

'Well, I'd like to think it was someone local,' said the Superintendent. 'It'ud make our job a wee bit easier. But we can't count on it — not until we know a good bit more than we do at present . . . '

The door was pushed open and Linda, looking more untidy than usual in a black dress that appeared to have most of the buttons off, announced without preliminary:

'Sir Robert Stanton wants to see you.'

'Oh,' the vicar sounded a trifle surprised. 'Wants to see me? Where — er — have you put him, Linda?'

' 'E's waiting in the hall,' answered Linda. 'Shall I bring 'im in?'

'Who is Sir Robert Stanton, sir?' inquired MacDonald. 'The name sounds familiar.'

'Our local bigwig,' said Mortimer. 'Owns most of the land and property round here.'

'He owns the cottage Miss Shand lived in, sir,' augmented Inspector Blane.

'Does he indeed,' said the Superintendent with sudden interest. 'I'd rather like to have a word with him, sir.'

'Show Sir Robert in here, Linda,' said Armitage.

Linda nodded and departed.

'I cannot imagine what he wants to see me about,' murmured the vicar, wrinkling his forehead.

'Curiosity, probably,' remarked Doctor Mortimer. 'Heard about the key, I expect. Very old family the Stantons. There was a Stanton at the Manor when the third George was on the throne. There's only Sir Robert, his brother Richard, and Lady Stanton, left now . . . '

'No children?' asked MacDonald.

'No,' said Mortimer shaking his head. 'There's a cousin living with them — young fellow named Ferrall . . . '

He broke off as the door opened again and Linda ushered in a thick-set man with close-cropped grey hair and a clipped moustache of the same hue. Sir Robert Stanton was dressed immaculately in rough tweeds, despite the heat of the afternoon, and looked the epitome of a retired Colonel.

'Afternoon, Armitage,' he greeted in a slightly hoarse voice. 'Sorry to disturb you like this, but I've just heard about this terrible affair — the Shand woman, I mean . . . ' He became aware of the other people in the room and nodded to Mortimer and Blane. 'Oh, how d'ye do, Mortimer, how d'ye do, Inspector . . . '

'Sit down, Sir Robert,' said Armitage. He introduced the superintendent. But Sir Robert refused the offer to sit down. Restlessly he moved about the big room, talking all the time.

'I couldn't believe it when they told me,' he said, frowning and fingering his moustache. 'Dreadful thing to have happened, eh? Shocking. Is it true she was strangled?'

'Quite true, sir,' answered MacDonald.

'Terrible, terrible,' muttered Sir Robert. 'Suppose there hasn't been time for you to form any idea who was responsible, eh?'

'Well, hardly, sir,' said the superintendent.

'Do sit down, Sir Robert,' said Armitage again, but the grey-haired man shook his head impatiently.

'No, no, can't stay very long. Only dropped in to get the truth about this thing . . . Dreadful thing to happen in Lesser Sweeping, eh? I suppose she was the type of woman these things *do* happen to. No morals, loose living, and all that . . . Quite an ordinary sort of crime, I imagine, eh? Nasty business, though . . . You'll probably find it was one of the people she used to have down to stay with her . . . Appalling crowd — capable of anything, in my opinion . . .'

He was talking jerkily and unevenly. There was, thought MacDonald, very little doubt that Sir Robert Stanton was labouring under some intense agitation. A far greater agitation than the matter seemed to warrant.

'Might be a lunatic,' said Mortimer gruffly.

38

Sir Robert stopped dead and swung round toward him. His tanned face had gone curiously mottled.

'What's that?' he said thickly. 'A lunatic . . . What makes you think that, eh?'

'It's that type of crime,' answered the doctor. 'Don't you agree, Superintendent?'

'Could be, sir,' assented MacDonald cautiously.

'You've no definite grounds for believing it to be a lunatic, have you?' demanded Sir Robert quickly.

MacDonald shook his head.

'We've no definite grounds yet to go on at all, sir,' he said.

The colour came back slowly to Sir Robert's cheeks. He thrust his hands into his pockets.

'In my opinion,' he declared, 'jealousy's at the bottom of it. That's the motive, I'll be bound. Much more likely, eh? Some man who thought he was the only pebble on the beach and found out he wasn't. Depend upon it, you'll find I'm right . . . '

'Maybe, sir,' said MacDonald noncommittally.

A hail from outside the open French windows made them all look up. A fair-haired man with a long and slightly vacuous face that bore a friendly grin stepped across the threshold.

'Hello, hello,' he greeted in a rather high-pitched voice. 'I say, I hope I'm not intruding on a summit conference or anything like that, but I saw that the jolly old windows were open and it seemed a fearful waste of time to go round to the front door when all one had to do was pop across the lawn.'

His grin broadened as he looked affably from one to the other.

'Oh, come in, Payne,' invited the vicar. 'You know everybody except Superintendent MacDonald, I think. Superintendent — Mr. Ronald Payne.'

'How do you do, sir,' said MacDonald politely.

'Absolutely brimming over with the joy of life, old chap,' said Mr. Payne, leaning up against the window frame. 'I suppose you're on the job, eh? I say, this is a bit of a knock-out, isn't it? Notoriety comes to Lesser Sweeping, eh? Terrific rush by all the Sunday newspapers to outdo each other with the gory details, eh?'

'It *is* murder, you know, Payne,' admonished Armitage. 'There's nothing really very humorous about it.'

'I entirely agree,' put in Sir Robert with a look of strong disapproval. 'Not the kind of thing to be funny about.'

The grin on the face of Mr. Payne vanished and was replaced by an expression of deep concern.

'Oh, I say, look here, you know,' he expostulated. 'I'm not trying to be funny, you know. I'm being absolutely serious. Not a spark of humour in the old chassis — not a spark.'

'You've got an unfortunate way of expressing yourself,' grunted Mortimer.

Ronald Payne turned toward him with a slightly injured expression on his vacuous face.

'Oh, look here, dash it all, what have I said?' he demanded unhappily. 'It stands to reason that you can't have women being strangled about the place without causing a pretty nifty stir, now *can* you?'

'Only *one* woman has been strangled

— so far as we know,' said Superintendent MacDonald with a faint smile.

'I know,' said Payne. 'I was only speaking figuratively. I don't mind telling you,' he went on conversationally, 'that the whole village is simply sizzling with excitement — absolutely brimming over.'

'I can well believe it,' grunted the doctor.

'Rumours are humming about like swarms of demented bees,' continued Payne. 'That's why I meandered along — to see if I could pick up the real gen.'

'I'm afraid there's nothing we can tell you, sir,' said MacDonald.

'All very hush-hush and top-secret, eh?' said Payne. 'Pity. I was hoping to get hold of a few juicy details to tell Betty. She's frightfully interested, you know. All agoggle, if you get me.'

'How is your wife today?' asked Doctor Mortimer.

'A bit more chirpy, I'm glad to say,' answered Payne. 'She's getting up this afternoon . . . '

'Tell her not to stay up too long,' warned Mortimer. 'Three hours at the most. I'll call in and see her this evening.'

'Okay, I'll tell her.' Payne regarded them each in turn, apparently hoping that somebody would say something. But a rather stony silence was all that greeted him and he sighed.

'I seem to be a bit *de trop* and all that,' he remarked at length. 'I'll pop in again when the climate's hotter, eh?'

'I'm afraid,' said the vicar, 'that we are all rather disturbed and upset by what has happened . . . '

'No need to apologise, padre,' interrupted Payne. 'Really shouldn't have come barging in like a bumble bee in a bottle, eh? No offence given or taken, as they say.'

'No, no,' said Armitage hastily, 'I didn't mean . . . '

Payne grinned.

''Stay not upon the order of thy going . . . ' and all that stuff, eh?' he said. 'That's me. Well, bye-bye for now. You can open up your hearts in perfect safety, secure in the knowledge that the cuckoo has fled from the nest.'

He waved a vague hand at them and ambled off across the lawn.

4

There was a short silence after he had gone, broken by a sound that was suspiciously like a snort from Sir Robert Stanton.

'How a sensible woman like Elizabeth Selby ever came to marry a brainless young ass like that is beyond my comprehension,' he declared.

'He's quite a good-hearted fellow,' said the Reverend Colin Armitage. 'It's only his manner . . . '

'That infernally inane chatter,' growled Sir Robert. 'Gets on your nerves. His wife has my sympathy.'

'She doesn't need it, you know,' said Doctor Mortimer, mopping at his face again. 'Very devoted couple those two . . . '

'I gather, from what you said just now, sir,' said MacDonald, 'that Mrs. Payne is an invalid?'

Doctor Mortimer nodded.

'Heart,' he answered briefly. 'Nothing

to be done for it — except rest as much as possible . . . '

Sir Robert glanced at his watch.

'By jove!' he ejaculated. 'No idea it was so late. I must be off. Got to get over to Midchester and see some horses . . . '

'We must be going too, sir,' put in Superintendent MacDonald, rising to his feet. 'You'll be hearing from the Coroner's Officer about the inquest, sir — and you too, doctor.'

'I suppose it will be quite a short affair, eh?' asked Sir Robert.

'Just evidence of identification and the medical evidence, I expect, sir,' answered MacDonald. 'We shall ask for an adjournment — unless, of course, anything further comes to light in the meanwhile.'

'I'd be glad . . . ' Sir Robert had an unusual diffidence and hesitation in his voice. 'I'd be glad if — if you'd let me know of any — any developments, superintendent.'

'I've no doubt you'll hear if there are, sir,' answered MacDonald noncommittally. 'Goodbye, Mr. Armitage.'

The vicar rose from behind the writing

table. There was a thoughtful pucker between his eyes, and his manner was a little more absent-minded than usual.

'Oh — er — yes, goodbye, goodbye . . . '

'Mind if we go this way, sir?' asked the superintendent, jerking his head toward the open French windows. 'Save disturbing the household.'

'Certainly, certainly, if you wish . . . ' Armitage sat down again and began to fiddle with a pencil. 'If there's anything I can do . . . '

'We'll let you know, sir,' said the superintendent; and, with a nod all round, he took his departure, followed by Inspector Blane.

'Seems quite a capable fellow,' remarked Sir Robert, following their retreating figures with his eyes — rather troubled eyes they seemed to Doctor Mortimer. 'Not giving much away, though, eh?'

'Not very much to give away at present,' said Mortimer.

'No — no, I suppose not,' agreed Sir Robert. 'I wonder if they'll get the person who did it, eh?'

'They usually do,' grunted the doctor.

'Very glad when it's all cleared up,' said Sir Robert. He passed a plump hand over his short grey hair, wearily. 'Very worrying and unpleasant knowing there's a murderer at large somewhere, eh? Oh, well, I must be off. May as well go this way, too. Bye . . . bye, Armitage.'

'Goodbye, Sir Robert,' said the vicar. 'Oh, by the way, I hope your brother is better.'

Sir Robert, who was on the point of going out of the window, swung round sharply.

'Better?' he demanded. 'What d'you mean — better?'

'My daughter saw him in the village the other day,' explained Armitage, 'and she said he was looking very ill . . . '

'Nonsense!' retorted Sir Robert angrily. 'Nothing the matter with him at all — never better in his life . . . Let me know if you hear anything more about this horrible business. Always get me on the phone, you know. Must go now, or I shall be devilish late.'

He strode quickly out the window and

walked away rapidly across the lawn.

Doctor Mortimer uttered a low whistle.

'He seems mighty perturbed about this murder,' he remarked.

'I suppose it's only natural that he should be interested,' said the vicar, running the pencil up and down his blotting pad. 'After all, the dead woman was one of his tenants . . . '

'You think that was the reason? Because I don't,' said the doctor, shaking his head. 'He was more interested than that would warrant. He's in a very bad nervous state, Armitage. He tried to hide it, but you can't fool a doctor. Look at the way he snapped your head off about his brother.'

'Yes, I was rather surprised.'

'There *is* something the matter with Richard Stanton, you know,' declared Mortimer. 'I don't care what his brother says. I've seen him about, and he's definitely ill.'

'That's what Merle said,' replied Armitage. 'I can't understand why Sir Robert should deny it.'

'Curious, eh?' said Mortimer. He got up out of the deep easy chair with difficulty. 'Well, can't stop here gossiping. Still got a couple of patients to visit. Regular old hypochondriacs — nothing the matter with either of 'em really, but they get annoyed if I don't pop in and listen to their complaints.'

'Give our fondest regards to Mrs. Payne when you see her this evening,' said the vicar.

'I will,' said Doctor Mortimer. 'By jove, it's hot. I suppose we're in for a spell of this weather. Can't say I like it. If I don't see you before, we shall meet at the inquest, I suppose?'

'Yes. An unpleasant ordeal but unavoidable,' said Armitage.

'Oh, well, it'll be pretty short, I've no doubt. Goodbye for the present.'

Mopping his face vigorously with his handkerchief, Doctor Mortimer went lumbering away to his car which he had left outside the garden gate.

The Reverend Colin Armitage leaned back in his chair and gently stroked his forehead with the first and second fingers of his right hand. He looked rather tired and there was a strained expression on his thin face. Frowning, he stared up at the discoloured ceiling . . .

Merle, coming in to call him for tea, thought he was asleep because she had to speak to him twice before he answered her.

'Tea?' he said vaguely. 'Oh, yes, my dear . . . yes certainly.'

'You look a bit under the weather, Daddy.' said Merle. She perched herself on the arm of his chair and slid her arm round his neck. 'What's the matter?'

'It's been a very trying day, my dear,' said her father. He sighed.

'Is there any fresh news?' asked Merle curiously.

The vicar shook his head.

'What did Sir Robert come for?' she asked. 'Just vulgar curiosity?'

'I suppose you could call it that . . . Yes, I suppose that's really what it was, though it struck me that there was, perhaps, something more . . . I've no doubt that the entire population of the village will find some pretext for calling.' Again the vicar sighed. 'The Sunday School Teachers' preparation class this evening will, I am sure, be unusually well attended.'

Merle laughed.

'You can't blame people for being curious, Daddy,' she said. 'It's the most exciting thing that's happened here for years. I know, it's not a very nice way of looking at it, but everybody's interested in a murder and this is the first that's happened on the doorstep . . . '

'Yes, yes . . . the first,' murmured the vicar.

'What *is* the matter, Daddy?' asked Merle anxiously.

'Matter, my dear?' Armitage reached up and patted the hand that rested on his shoulder. 'Nothing, nothing . . . '

'Oh, yes there is,' declared his daughter, peering at him critically. 'Something's worrying you. What is it?'

'I'm — I'm a little uneasy, my dear,' he answered. 'Yes — a little uneasy.'

'Why?' she demanded.

He considered for several seconds before he answered her. At last he said, slowly:

'The message, Merle. The message that

was sent to me with the key. It troubles me. I don't know whether Superintendent MacDonald has seen the significance of it. I feel that he must have . . . Perhaps I ought to have drawn his attention to it . . . '

'What do you mean, Daddy?' asked Merle.

'You remember how it was worded?'

' "This is Bluebeard's first key." That was it, wasn't it?' she said.

'That was it,' he answered. 'Don't you see what it implies?'

'Implies?' She wrinkled her forehead in perplexity.

'If someone sends you a — box of chocolates, shall we say? They don't say, 'This is the first box of chocolates' unless . . . ' He paused and looked up at her.

A look of horrified understanding came into her face.

'Unless they are going to send me — *another*,' she whispered huskily.

'Or others,' said the Reverend Colin Armitage. 'Exactly. That's why I'm uneasy, Merle. I'm afraid, desperately afraid, that there may be — others . . . '

5

Ronald Payne had spoken no more than the truth when he said that the village of Lesser Sweeping was seething with excitement over the murder of Sylvia Shand. It was the sole topic of conversation whenever two or more of the inhabitants met, either in their own homes, at the Stanton Arms, or shopping in the High Street.

The dead woman had been heartily disliked, and the general reaction to her death was summed up by Mrs. Dawlish over the garden wall to her neighbour.

'Good riddance to bad rubbish, that's what I say,' she declared. 'You mark my words, women like that always come to a bad end. They are born with evil in 'em and they die in an evil way.'

Curiously enough, Superintendent Mac-Donald was saying much the same thing to Inspector Blane in his office at the police station in Midchester.

'The main clue to this case will be found in the history of the dead woman herself, Blane,' he said, looking at his subordinate through clouds of smoke from his battered pipe. 'That's what we've got to trace out. Who was she? Where did she come from? What was her background? And why, above all things, did she rent that cottage in Lesser Sweeping for the summer? It's not the sort of place that a woman like that would choose.'

'I agree with you there, sir,' said the inspector. 'Puzzled a lot of people that did.'

'Either she was hiding up from something, or someone, or else she came there because there was someone in the district she wanted to meet,' said MacDonald. 'I don't suppose we shall find that her name was Shand at all. It doesn't ring true, somehow. Sylvia Shand. It's like a film star.'

'If it wasn't her name, sir,' remarked the inspector, 'It's going to be a bit difficult tracing her back.'

'She gave a banker's reference, and a solicitor's reference, to Sir Robert's agents when she took the cottage. Maybe something will come of those. Sergeant Mathews is looking into that.' He took the pipe from between his lips and stared into the reeking bowl. 'I'm rather puzzled over Sir Robert,' he continued thoughtfully. 'Much more bothered about the murder than you'd expect from a gentleman of his type. All dithery about it, it struck me. There might be something there, you know. Not the kind of person he'd normally let a cottage to, eh?'

'You're right there, sir,' said Blane. 'But I expect he didn't know what she was like until it was all fixed up.'

'That may be right,' answered Mac-Donald thoughtfully. 'All the same, that doesn't account for the state of nerves he was in when he called at the Vicarage the other afternoon. I think there's something there well worth looking into.'

'The Stantons are a very old family, sir,' said the inspector. 'I shouldn't think . . . '

'You never can tell with these old families, Blane,' said the Superintendent, shaking his head. 'All sorts of things buried. There's a brother, isn't there?'

'Mr. Richard,' answered Blane. 'He's been away for a couple of years or so in South Africa. Only came back a week or so ago . . . '

'What was he doing in South Africa?' asked MacDonald, but Blane had to admit that he did not know. 'The thing we've got to decide, and it's not going to be easy, is whether this is a local crime, or someone out of the woman's past. It's going to save a great deal of work and trouble if it turns out to be local. If we've got to trace out all the people she knew, and find out where they were at the time she was strangled, it's going to take the devil of a long time.'

There was a tap on the office door and Detective Sergeant Mathews came in. He was a thick-set man with a round, reddish face that usually beamed with good nature. Today he was looking anything but pleased.

'Drawn a blank at the bank, sir,' he said. 'The woman only opened her account a month before she came to live in Lesser Sweeping. She paid in five hundred pounds in cash. They had to give her a reference, of course . . . '

'But the manager doesn't know anything else about her, eh?' said MacDonald. He grunted. 'Didn't they want the usual introduction, or reference, themselves?'

'She supplied one,' answered Mathews. 'A hair-dressing salon in London. *Maison de Vaux*. They bank at the Regent Street branch of the same bank.'

'Ah,' said MacDonald alertly. 'Now, there may be something there . . . '

'That's what I thought, sir,' said Mathews, 'but there isn't. I got on to the manager of this salon, or whatever you call it. He'd heard of Sylvia Shand, right enough. She was a client of the place. But he knew nothing about her, except that she'd told him one day that she was going to rent a cottage in the country and she wanted to open a banking account in Midchester. She said she'd never had one before and could he give her a letter to *his* bank. Rather foolishly he did. She was a client, and a good one, and he wanted to oblige her.'

'Can't blame him really, I suppose,'

said the superintendent. 'After all, he wasn't letting himself in for anything. Not very difficult to get references, you know. The whole thing's a farce, when you come to think of it. Um. Well that's that. What about the solicitor?'

'That's a wash-out too, sir,' answered Mathews. 'Dodson and Wright. They've got an office off the High Street here. I saw Mr. Dodson and he's never heard of Sylvia Shand in his life . . . '

'Never heard of her?' echoed MacDonald. 'But man alive, he gave her a reference. You've got the letter. We got it from Sir Robert's agent . . . '

'I know all that, sir,' replied the sergeant. 'I showed it to Mr. Dodson. But he swears it was never sent by his firm.'

'Then who the devil *did* send it?' demanded the superintendent. 'It's on headed paper and it must have been in reply to a letter sent by Sir Robert's agent . . . '

'There's no record of any such letter in the office,' declared Mathews. 'Mr. Dodson went through all the files for that date. No letter was received from Sir Robert's agent about Sylvia Shand . . . '

'She seems to have been mighty careful to cover her tracks, sir,' remarked Blane.

'She certainly has,' agreed MacDonald. He knocked the ashes out of his pipe and proceeded to refill it from a shabby pouch. 'We've just got to uncover 'em, that's all. That's the most important thing. We can't get very far until we know more about the dead woman. Was she married? I'm inclined to believe that there is, or was, a husband somewhere . . . '

'Maybe the photographs 'ull bring in some information,' said Blane, hopefully.

'If anyone can recognise the woman from them,' answered the superintendent. 'Strangulation doesn't improve the appearance. Still we must hope for the best. Maybe the Yard will be able to tell us something. In the meanwhile, we'd better see what we can discover from the inhabitants of Lesser Sweeping. We'll make a start with Sir Robert Stanton . . . '

★   ★   ★

The Manor was a large and beautiful old house of mellow brick, with twisted chimneys and mullioned windows. It stood on the outskirts of the village in well-kept gardens and parkland. The drive, winding between an avenue of plain trees and banks of rhododendrons, now in the full glory of bloom, led up to the main front door — a massive affair of iron-bound oak under a projecting porch.

Inspector Blane brought the police car to a gentle stop in front of this imposing entrance, and he and Superintendent Mac-Donald got out. They mounted the flight of narrow, worn stone steps and pulled at a wrought iron bell-pull. There was no sound of any bell ringing within the house, but, after a few seconds, the big door was opened by an elderly maidservant.

Superintendent MacDonald stated his name and business and asked to see Sir Robert. The servant ushered them into a wide hall and went away. In a few minutes she came back.

'This way please,' she said, and led them across the hall to a door on the right. As she put her hand on the handle, a door on the other side of the hall opened and a man came quickly out. He was a short, lean man with a pale, lined face. His deep-set eyes moved over them with a queer flickering, uneasy expression, and a muscle at the side of his mouth jerked spasmodically. The man was a bundle of jangling nerves.

He turned abruptly, went back into the room from which he had just emerged, and hurriedly shut the door. But Mac-Donald had seen something else apart from the nervous twitching of the mouth.

There had come a sudden expression into those deep-set eyes which was more than uneasiness — a look of stark, naked fear.

The room they were shown into was a long, cool drawing-room. It was a large and beautifully appointed room with many deep-cushioned chairs and great bowls full of flowers. The pale green walls were hung with a number of oil paintings — portraits of generations of Stantons — and interspersed with crystal wall-brackets that matched the big centre chandelier.

'Will you wait here, please,' said the maidservant. 'Sir Robert will not keep you long.'

She withdrew, closing the door behind her.

'Who was the man in the hall?' asked MacDonald as soon as she had gone.

'That was Mr. Richard Stanton, sir,' answered Inspector Blane. 'He's the one who's just come back from South Africa.'

'South Africa? Um, yes, I remember now.' MacDonald frowned and stared up at a portrait over the mantelpiece. 'Rather pale for someone who's just come back from a hot climate, eh?'

'Perhaps he didn't go out in the sun much, sir, while he was there?' suggested Blane, to which the superintendent made no reply.

Sir Robert Stanton did not keep them waiting long. He came in quickly, greeted them politely, and said abruptly: 'I can't imagine why you should want to see me. Unless you have some further news?'

'I'm afraid not, sir,' said MacDonald. 'Nothing fresh has come to light at the moment. But you will understand that in a case like this there are certain routine inquiries that have to be made . . . '

'Yes, yes, I understand all that,'

interrupted Sir Robert impatiently. 'But why come to me? I can't help you in any way. I knew nothing about the woman — nothing at all.'

'You never met her, sir?' asked the superintendent.

'No. I've seen her once or twice in the village, that's all,' answered Sir Robert. 'I had no wish to become further acquainted with a woman of that type. I was extremely annoyed when I found that my agent had let her the cottage. Unfortunately, he had no idea what she was like until it was too late. A most undesirable person in every way.'

'Quite so, sir,' agreed MacDonald. 'I understand that that is the opinion of most of the people here. But if this should turn out to be a *local* crime . . . '

Sir Robert dismissed the possibility with a wave of his hand.

'I don't for a moment believe that it is,' he declared emphatically. 'You'll only be wasting your time if you go to work on those lines. You can take it from me that the person who killed her was one of her disreputable friends who used to come and see her. That's where you'd better look . . . '

'That's just the difficulty, sir,' said the superintendent. 'We don't know who these people are, or anything about them . . . '

'It's your business to find out,' snapped Sir Robert. 'As I've told you it is no good coming to *me*. I know nothing.'

'Quite so, sir,' said MacDonald again. 'I'm inclined to agree with you that it was one of her friends who killed her. At the same time, you'll understand, we've got to cover all eventualities. Now, is there anyone in the neighbourhood with whom she might have been acquainted?'

'Extremely unlikely.' Sir Robert shook his head. 'It's not the slightest use your wasting your time questioning *me* about the woman. If, and when, you have come to any conclusion about the matter I shall be very glad to hear about it. Until then I really must decline to be bothered about it.'

There was a note of dismissal in his voice, but MacDonald was not to be got rid of so easily.

'Would it be possible, while we are here, sir,' he said, 'to have a word with your brother, Mr. Richard Stanton?'

The colour receded from Sir Richard's cheeks, leaving them a pasty yellow. He drew in his breath sharply like a man who had received a sudden and unexpected blow.

'Why should you wish to see my brother?' he asked in a voice that was curiously husky and unsteady.

'I understand that he is in the habit of going for long walks,' said the superintendent. 'I wondered if, by any chance, he might have seen anyone talking to the dead woman at any time or . . . '

'He can tell you nothing — nothing at all,' asserted Sir Robert. 'He knows no more than I do. In any case he is not at home at the moment.'

And that's a deliberate lie, thought MacDonald. For some reason best known to himself, Sir Robert Stanton did not want them to interview his brother. There was something decidedly fishy here. Was it possible that Richard Stanton *had* known the dead woman? If so, he must have made her acquaintance during the short time between his return from South Africa and her death. He remembered the pale, twitching face, and the flickering shifty eyes. Was Richard Stanton's obviously nervous condition the result of Sylvia Shand's murder? Had he, perhaps, known her before he had gone abroad, and renewed the friendship, or whatever it was, in Lesser Sweeping?

Superintendent MacDonald was a very thoughtful man as he took leave of Sir Robert and went back to the police car. There was definitely something here that would be worth looking into.

He had seen fear in the eyes of Richard Stanton and he had seen a reflection of that fear in the eyes of his brother.

6

Superintendent MacDonald's next call was at White Lodge, the home of Ronald Payne. He did not expect that the visit would yield any results, but he had made a list of everybody in the village and was determined to omit no one, however unlikely, who might be able to supply the smallest tittle to his meagre stock of information.

Mr. Payne was sitting on the low, rose-covered veranda in a cushioned basket chair talking to a young man with very black hair and a bronzed face — a very good-looking young man indeed — and a woman who, in spite of the fact that her first youth had faded, was still pretty in a wan and rather anaemic fashion.

Ronald Payne introduced the young man as Michael Ferrall, and the woman as his own wife.

'Come and join the happy family,' he

said. 'Park the old bods and quaff a jorum.' He went over to a table laden with drinks. 'What's it to be? Just say the word and — abracadabra! — Ronaldo Paynovitch will produce the goods.'

'Well, that's very kind of you, sir,' said MacDonald. 'Perhaps just a wee drop of Scotch . . . '

'The golden wine of Scotland, eh?' cried Payne, busy among the bottles and glasses. 'What about you, Inspector?'

'I'd like some beer, if it's all the same to you, sir,' said the inspector.

'Beer it shall be. You want the best beer, we have it?' said Payne. 'How's the local sensation, eh? Clues flowing in from all directions?' He came over and thrust a cold tumbler into the superintendent's willing hand. MacDonald shook his head.

'I'm afraid we haven't made much headway at present,' he said, sipping his drink appreciatively. 'We wondered if you might be able to supply us with any useful information.'

Ronald Payne turned from giving Inspector Blane his beer with a look of surprise on his vacuous face.

'Me?' he ejaculated. 'Struck the wrong shop absolutely, old chap. Positively barren of any knowledge whatsoever.'

'Why,' said Elizabeth Payne, in a soft and altogether delightful voice, 'should you believe that my husband could give you any information about this horrible business?'

'We are trying everybody, ma'am,' answered MacDonald. 'It's just a question of the usual routine.'

'Rather a tedious job, isn't it?' remarked Michael Ferrall. 'I mean, if you're going to interview everybody in the village.'

'Police work is mostly tedious, sir,' said the superintendent. 'A question of seeing people and hoping that they'll be able to give you a line . . . '

'Picked the wrong number out of the hat with me,' said Payne, shaking his head. 'Dash it all, what should *I* know?'

'You never met the dead woman, sir?' asked MacDonald.

'Good lord, no,' exclaimed Payne with a note of horror in his voice at the bare idea. 'Not my type at all, eh, Betty?' He smiled at his wife.

'Definitely not — from what I've heard about her,' answered Elizabeth Payne, smiling back at him.

'I wasn't suggesting, sir,' said MacDonald, 'that you were friendly. I just wondered if, maybe, you might have met her at some time or other.'

'Nothing doing, old top,' said Payne. 'The lady didn't go out much, you know. One of the hot-house flowers, eh?'

'Did you ever see any of these friends who used to visit her?' asked the superintendent.

'By jove, yes,' cried Payne. 'Now, I *have* seen two or three of those birds. And jolly queer birds, too. You remember me telling you, Betty? About those two types at the local?'

Mrs. Payne laughed.

'All long hair, dirty finger nails, and Art with a capital 'A',' continued Ronald Payne. 'When you got past all the face fungus and the trimmings, there was nothing there!'

Inspector Blane looked a little astonished.

'Nothing there?' he repeated.

'He means that it was all show,' said

MacDonald. 'Isn't that right, Mr. Payne?'

'That's what I said,' said Payne. 'All camouflage, old boy. Knew no more about art than a blind peke! They could put away the booze, though. Pink gins by the dozen.' He lifted his hand several times to his lips in quick succession. 'Got as sozzled as coots.'

'Were they regular visitors to the dead woman?' asked MacDonald.

'Couldn't tell you,' said Payne, shaking his head. 'Only saw them that once. Don't often go into the old boozer, do I, Betty? Was staggering past that morning and happened to drop in. Saw one of the female of the species in the High Street. What they say is quite right, you know. Far worse than the male, old fruit! Never seen anything like it. Couldn't have had any bones! All undulating like a snake.' He gave an exaggerated imitation of the woman's walk which made his wife laugh and drew a dry smile from MacDonald. 'Straight hair the colour of tow, and a whole shopful of cosmetics. You could smell the different perfumes across the street, but her friends had never told her.'

'You are an ass, Ronald,' said Ferrall, laughing.

'I was only doing my best to describe 'em to the superintendent,' expostulated Payne.

'And a very good description too, sir,' said MacDonald. 'I mind the type well. Mr. Ferrall, you are Sir Robert Stanton's agent, I understand.'

'That's correct,' said Ferrall.

'Was it you who took up the dead woman's references?'

Ferrall nodded.

'I've already seen your sergeant about that,' he said.

'I'm rather interested in this solicitor's reference,' said MacDonald. 'Apparently the solicitors state that they never received your letter?'

'They replied to it, anyway,' retorted Ferrall.

'I'm aware of that, sir,' said the superintendent. 'That is what puzzles me. Can you suggest how that could have happened?'

'Dogsbody,' said Ronald Payne.

'Eh?' MacDonald stared at him in surprise.

'Old Dodson had a clerk. Used to call him 'Dogsbody' — not old Dodson, me,' explained Payne. 'Didn't stop there long — got fired. Awful drip.'

'Well?' said MacDonald expectantly.

'That's the lot,' said Payne. 'The beautiful and seductive Sylvia gets a half-nelson on poor Dogsbody. Easiest thing in the world. Dropped handkerchief — sprained ankle, the old boloney. Dogsbody falls like a sputnik out of orbit. The thing's done. Bingo!'

'How do you know this?' asked the superintendent.

'Sheer deduction. You know my methods, Watson?' said Payne. 'Only solution. 'Eliminate the impossible and whatever remains, however improbable, must be the truth.' Clever chap, old Sherlock.'

It was quite obvious that Inspector Blane was completely out of his depth. He looked from one to the other with the rather helpless look of a dog who is not certain what his master means.

'H'm,' remarked MacDonald. 'You think this fellow — what was his name, by the way?'

'Dickson,' put in Ferrall. 'Charles Dickson.'

'You think this clerk, Charles Dickson, may have intercepted the letter you sent, Mr. Ferrall, and replied to it himself?'

'Right out of the jolly old biscuit tin,' said Payne.

'I think you're probably right, Ronnie,' said Ferrall. 'Dickson was a bit of a wet week. He'd have fallen for anything.'

'He was dismissed?' asked the superintendent.

'Yes,' replied Ferrall. 'Just for incompetence — nothing serious.'

'I call incompetence jolly serious,' said Payne.

'You should know,' retorted Ferrall.

'Oh, I say, look here,' remonstrated Payne. 'Are you suggesting that there's anything incompetent about me, old bean?'

'I'm sure nobody could,' put in his wife. The smile she gave him was full of affection. There was no doubt, thought MacDonald, that whatever anyone else might think, to his wife Ronald Payne was almost perfect.

'I take it,' he said, 'that this Dickson is a local man?'

'Oh, yes,' said Ferrall. 'He lives with his mother at number three The Cottages. It's a little cul-de-sac off the High Street.'

The superintendent made a note of the address and rose to his feet.

'We'll no bother you any more for the present,' he said.

'No bother,' said Payne. 'Wish I could produce the old clues for you. The spirit is willing but the flesh is weak. Sure you won't have another spot?'

Inspector Blane looked as if *he* would have liked some more beer, but his superior declined, so he had to follow suit. They went back to the waiting car.

'Bit of a chump that chap Payne,' said Blane, as they got in.

'Not very bright,' answered MacDonald, 'but he seems to be a good-hearted fellow. His wife evidently thinks a lot of him.'

'Very nice woman, Mrs. Payne,' said Blane. 'It's a pity she's an invalid.'

'Aye,' agreed the superintendent. 'She's still attractive. I'd say she was just the right woman for young Payne. He needs mothering, and I think he gets it.'

'Are you going to see this chap, Dickson, sir?' asked the inspector, as they drove in the direction of the High Street.

MacDonald nodded.

'We may as well get that point cleared up,' he said. 'There's always the chance, too, that he might be able to tell us something useful.'

The Cottages consisted of four small and rather old-fashioned houses set along one side of a narrow road that ended in a high brick wall. They were all very neat, the front doors opening directly onto the pavement.

Number three was more dingy than the others. Most of them had window boxes full of geraniums and petunias, but number three was without embellishment.

MacDonald knocked.

There was a long pause, and then the door was opened by an untidy woman, with her sleeves rolled up above her elbows, and her hands showing traces of soapsuds.

'Mrs. Dickson?' inquired MacDonald pleasantly.

The woman looked surprised and, he

thought, rather uneasy.

'That's right,' she said. 'If it's about the telly, I . . . '

'It's nothing to do with television,' interrupted the superintendent. 'I should like to see your son, if he's available.'

The uneasiness changed to definite alarm.

'Who are you?' she asked, suspiciously.

'I'm Superintendent MacDonald of the C.I.D. Midchester,' said MacDonald. 'I'm making inquiries into the murder of a woman called Sylvia Shand . . . '

'What's my son got to do with it?' she demanded harshly.

'I understand,' said MacDonald, 'that he was recently working at Dodson and Wright's, the solicitors . . . '

'What if he was?' she broke in. 'What's that got to do with it?'

'I just want to ask him a few questions,' said the superintendent.

'What is it, mother?' called a thin, high-pitched voice from somewhere inside the cottage.

'The police want to see you, Charlie,' answered his mother. She turned to

MacDonald. 'You'd better come in,' she said grudgingly.

The front door opened directly into the small sitting-room which was poorly furnished and incredibly untidy. As they entered, a youth appeared through a door at the other end. He was a thin, weedy youth with a shock of tangled fair hair and a rather pimply face. There was a lurking expression of fear in his small eyes.

'What's it all about?' he demanded a little truculently.

'You are Mr. Charles Dickson?' asked MacDonald, and the youth nodded. 'You knew Miss Sylvia Shand, the woman who was strangled, I believe?' said the superintendent.

'Who said I knew 'er?' demanded the youth.

'Did you or didn't you?' snapped MacDonald curtly.

'I spoke to 'er once or twice,' admitted Dickson, 'but I didn't know anything about her. What's the idea?'

'Miss Shand gave as a reference, when she was taking her cottage, the firm of

Dodson and Wright,' said MacDonald. 'They gave her a reference in reply to a letter from Mr. Ferrall, Sir Robert Stanton's agent . . . '

'Well?' demanded the youth as he paused.

'I am informed by Mr. Dodson, that he knows nothing about such a reference,' continued the superintendent. 'He never saw the letter from Sir Robert Stanton's agent. I believe you can explain how that was?'

'It's got nothing to do with me,' began Dickson, but MacDonald cut him short.

'It's got a lot to do with you,' he said sternly. 'You intercepted the letter from Sir Robert's agent, didn't you, and sent your own reply, typed on Dodson and Wright's headed paper? That's what it's got to do with you.'

The youth crumpled.

'I didn't see there was any harm,' he muttered.

'How did it happen? How did you come to know the dead woman?' demanded Mac-Donald.

It was a simple story. Sylvia Shand had

met him in a teashop where he always went to have a sandwich and a cup of tea at lunch time. She had told him that she was taking a cottage in Lesser Sweeping, but that she couldn't find a solicitor's reference as she hadn't a solicitor. She had offered him five pounds to do what he did. He knew which letter it was because the envelope had the Stanton monogram on the flap.

'She was a nice lady,' ended Dickson. 'Said I ought to have a better job than just being a clerk. She was going to speak to some of her friends . . . '

The usual stuff, thought MacDonald. A combination of flattery and bribery. A whole lot of people with more intelligence than Dickson had fallen for those tactics — were falling every day.

'What else did you know about her?' he asked.

'Nothing at all,' declared the youth earnestly. 'I never saw her to speak to again. I left Dodson's soon after . . . '

'You never told me about this, Charlie,' snapped his mother, who had been listening anxiously. 'Getting mixed up with a woman like that . . . '

'Oh, stow it, Mother,' said Charlie ungraciously. 'I didn't get mixed up with 'er. I've told you all I did.'

'That was quite enough,' said the superintendent. 'Take my advice and don't do anything like that again. It's dishonest and you could get yourself into serious trouble.'

There was nothing more to be learned from Charlie Dickson. MacDonald questioned him closely concerning Sylvia Shand, but he came to the conclusion that the youth was speaking the truth. He didn't know anything more than he had said.

'Well,' said MacDonald as they climbed back in the car, 'we've cleared that up. I'm going back to Midchester to see if anything has come in about the woman. I'll drop you at the police station, here.'

There was nothing at Midchester. Superintendent MacDonald sat for a long time in his cheerless little office, pondering over the case and trying to decide what his next move should be. Obviously to trace the history of Sylvia Shand — if that was her real name, which he strongly doubted. What had been her background before she had rented the cottage in Lesser Sweeping? Where had she came from, and what had induced her to bury herself in such a rural district? It was not the sort of place to suit a woman like that at all. She must have had some very urgent reason for it. Was she afraid of someone? Was that why she had come — to hide? That seemed plausible, but who was the person, and what was she afraid of?

It would be difficult to discover that. The whole thing was difficult. And the key? What had induced the murderer to send that to the Reverend Colin Armitage? Sheer bravado, or was there something significant about it?

Again, the woman might have come there because there was someone already living in the district that she wanted to be near. That was also a possibility that had to be taken into account.

MacDonald sighed as he prepared to go home to his wife and family. There was a lot to be done. On his way to his small, neat house on the outskirts of Midchester, he sketched out his plans for the following day. But he was destined never to put them into execution.

For the morning was to bring with it a fresh turn to the case, which made it even grimmer than it had been.

7

The second key reached the Reverend Colin Armitage by the first post. It was neatly packed, like the first, and inside was a slip of paper on which had been roughly printed in capital letters:

'THIS IS BLUEBEARD'S SECOND KEY'

The key this time was a Yale and a nearly new one.

When Merle had first seen the parcel, she had experienced a thrill that was not entirely unpleasant. She remembered her father's misgivings. He had expected that there would be a second key, and he had been right.

'Dear me, this is terrible, really terrible,' he said, staring at the key in his hand. 'I was afraid of it, but scarcely so soon ... Dear, dear, now to what lock does this key belong?'

But Merle couldn't help him this time.

There was no convenient cut, or anything else, by which to identify it.

The Reverend Colin Armitage telephoned to Inspector Blane, who, in turn, telephoned to Superintendent MacDonald, with the result that less than an hour after the vicar had received the key, they were both seated in his study at the Vicarage discussing this fresh development.

'I should have warned you,' said the vicar in a troubled voice. 'I should certainly have pointed out the possibility of this happening . . . '

'You expected this second key?' asked MacDonald in surprise.

'Yes, yes, of course,' answered the Reverend Colin Armitage. 'It was rather obvious, you see? I explained to my daughter . . . I'm surprised you didn't realise from the message . . . '

'I don't quite understand, sir,' said MacDonald.

Jerkily and very disjointedly, his mind evidently on something else, the vicar explained.

'I should have seen that,' agreed MacDonald frowning. 'The question is, who does this key belong to?'

'Yes, yes, a rather difficult problem,' said the vicar, stroking his forehead. 'There must be a considerable number of Yale keys in Lesser Sweeping. Dear me, it's really very interesting, you know . . . '

'I don't see how we're going to find out, sir,' remarked Inspector Blane. 'We can't go to everybody's house until we find . . . ' He broke off abruptly.

'Until we find somebody murdered, eh?' finished MacDonald. 'No, hardly . . . '

But they had no need to. There came, almost on the heels of the superintendent's remark, a telephone message. It came from Doctor Mortimer.

'Oh, got hold of you at last, have I,' he grunted over the wire, when the superintendent went to the telephone. 'They told me you were at the Vicarage when I got on to Midchester — both you and Blane. There's been another murder. Strangulation, same as the other. District nurse, this time. I'm there now; you'd better come as quickly as you can.'

MacDonald relayed the information to Blane and the vicar.

'Miss Cheeseman?' exclaimed Blane. 'She's only been here for a fortnight . . . '

'A very nice little woman,' said the Reverend Colin Armitage gravely. 'I should like to come along with you, if you wouldn't mind.'

'Aye, you can come, sir,' said Mac-Donald. 'I'll telephone the station at Midchester, if you don't mind, and then I'll be ready.'

Briefly he gave a number of orders over the telephone, and they hurried out to the waiting car.

The district nurse had occupied a comparatively new house at the end of a short street near the bottom of the High Street. It was a small house, scarcely more than a cottage, and the board at the side of the front door proclaimed who lived there in black letters on a white ground.

Doctor Mortimer's car stood outside the place when they drew up, and the doctor himself came out to the gate as they descended from the police car.

'Huh, better late than never,' he growled, mopping his face. 'You, too, Armitage, eh? This is a shocking business . . . shocking.

The other woman probably deserved what she got, but this poor soul . . . Strangled in her bed . . . dreadful . . . '

'How did you come to make the discovery, doctor?' asked MacDonald.

'Should have turned up on a case this morning — confinement. Didn't. I came to see what the matter was. Couldn't make anybody hear, but found the milk still on the step . . . '

'How did you get in, sir?' asked Blane.

'Smashed a window at the back,' said Mortimer with a scowl. 'Thought the blasted woman had overslept, or something. Found her in her bed . . . '

'We'd better go inside,' said Mac-Donald curtly. 'I hope you didn't disturb anything, doctor.'

'What do you take me for, a fool?' retorted Mortimer gruffly. 'How did you get in on this, Armitage. Get another key, eh?'

'What makes you think that?' asked the superintendent quickly.

'Brains,' answered Mortimer briefly.

'You're quite right, Mortimer,' said the vicar. 'It arrived by the first post this morning . . . '

'That means it was posted yesterday,' said Doctor Mortimer.

'It was,' agreed the vicar. 'It caught the last collection. The three-thirty collection . . . '

'Then the murderer must have posted it *before* he'd committed the crime,' said Mortimer. 'This poor woman wasn't dead, then . . . '

The Reverend Colin Armitage nodded.

'That had already struck me,' he confessed. 'A very significant point, don't you think?'

'You mean he'd already made up his mind . . . ?' began MacDonald.

'No, no,' said the vicar, shaking his head. '*That*, of course, but I was thinking about the key . . . '

Superintendent MacDonald uttered an irritated sound.

'Aye,' he said, 'I'm a fool not to've seen what you were driving at. He must have had the key in his possession at that time?'

'Exactly,' agreed Armitage.

They went up the stairs. It was a narrow staircase that exactly fitted the space between the walls of the hall.

Turning at the top, they walked along a passage, equally narrow, from which two doors opened.

'It's this one,' said Doctor Mortimer, lowering his voice unconsciously, and opening the first of the two.

It was a smallish room, overlooking the front of the house. The furniture was simple, consisting of a chest of drawers, a wardrobe, a single bed, and a small easy chair. There was a bedside table containing a glass of water and an alarm clock. A nurse's uniform lay across the chair, and on the top of the chest of drawers was a black case.

In the bed, or rather half in it and half sprawling on the floor, was the twisted body of a woman. She was about forty-five, with dark hair that was beginning to grey, and she was clad in a plain, white linen nightgown. Her face was congested and swollen, and, when they went closer, they could see, half buried in the flesh of the neck, a thin cord . . .

'A replica of the other,' murmured the vicar, peering down at the body. 'Dear me, this is really very dreadful . . .'

'It looks as though we've got a lunatic to deal with,' said MacDonald. 'When do you think she was killed, doctor?'

'Between the hours of twelve and two,' said Mortimer. 'I can't be more definite than that.'

Armitage was peering about the room in his absent, short-sighted manner, shaking his head gravely all the time. Near the foot of the wardrobe, he stooped and looked more intently at the floor.

'Have you found something, sir?' inquired MacDonald sharply.

'There appears to be something sticky here,' said the vicar.

The superintendent went over to his side. There was a tiny dark patch on the worn carpet. It looked as though a sweet had been trodden on. MacDonald took out a penknife and gently scraped the sticky substance into an old envelope.

'It's probably nothing of importance,' he remarked, 'but I'll have it examined and reported on. Most likely it's just a sweet that the woman dropped herself . . . '

There was a sound outside and presently there came a clattering of feet on the stairs. The photographers and the fingerprint men, whom MacDonald had telephoned for from the Vicarage, had arrived. They were followed by the police surgeon.

He made an examination of the body and confirmed the time of death. When he had finished, the photographers got busy and took a number of pictures from various angles suggested by MacDonald. The fingerprint men took over after this, and then the body was removed and carried down to the ambulance which had arrived in the meanwhile.

They went downstairs into the small, neatly furnished sitting-room.

'Now,' said MacDonald, sitting down at a small table, 'I should like you to tell me what you know about the dead woman. You say she'd only been here as district nurse for two weeks?'

Mortimer nodded.

'That's right. She took the place of old Miss Handford when she retired.'

'Where did she come from?' asked the superintendent.

'She was district nurse at Egglesfield, sir,' put in Inspector Blane. 'I believe, before that she was in London.'

'I know she was in the W.V.S. during the war,' said Doctor Mortimer. 'She told me so herself.'

'It shouldn't be difficult to trace her history,' said MacDonald. 'I'm wondering, do you see, if it links up anywhere with the Shand woman.'

'I should think that was very unlikely,' said Mortimer.

'Unlikely things happen, that's my experience,' said the superintendent. 'There's got to be a common motive for these two murders . . . '

'Unless they're the work of a homicidal maniac,' said Doctor Mortimer. 'It looks very like it to me.'

'And to me,' agreed MacDonald. 'But we can't take it for granted.'

'I should be interested to know how Bluebeard got hold of the key,' remarked the Reverend Colin Armitage thoughtfully.

'We're not sure yet that it *is* the key,' said the superintendent suddenly. 'Here, Blane, take it and see if it fits the lock.'

He took the key, which had already

been tested for prints without result, except for a few unidentifiable smudges, from his pocket and gave it to the inspector.

Blane went out into the hall and they heard him fumbling at the front door. He was back in a few seconds.

'It's the right key, sir,' he said.

'It's really remarkable how he could have got hold of it,' murmured the vicar. 'Unless, of course, it was a spare key . . . '

'Miss Cheeseman's handbag,' exclaimed MacDonald. 'It's probably upstairs somewhere. We'll have to go through all her things presently. See if you can find it, Blane.'

The inspector departed on this fresh errand.

'I'd like to exhaust everything else before we finally come to the lunatic theory,' said the superintendent. 'It seems to me that these crimes, however, are the work of a local person . . . '

'It's by no means conclusive,' said Armitage, shaking his head. 'Although, I'm inclined to agree with you. If it isn't a local person, it must be someone who is very familiar with the neighbourhood. As

I remarked before, that seems obvious from the key being sent to me . . . '

Blane came back carrying a rather shabby black handbag.

'Found it in the top drawer of the chest of drawers, sir,' he said, and handed it to MacDonald.

The superintendent opened it carefully and searched rapidly through the contents.

'Here we are,' he said, and produced a Yale key. He compared it with the other.

'Identical,' he announced. 'So it *was* the spare key that the murderer sent to you, vicar.' He frowned. 'Why did he send it? Why did he send the other?'

'I tell you, the man's got a kink,' said Mortimer. 'Not the action of a sane man.'

'It doesn't seem so, does it?' remarked the superintendent. 'Let's see if there's anything in this bag that might help us.'

He turned the contents of the handbag out on the table. There was nothing very much in it. A pair of spectacles in a case, a handkerchief, a small powder compact, a pair of nail scissors and a nail file, two receipted bills for stockings, and a small, black-covered book. MacDonald pounced on this and glanced quickly through it.

'It appears to be only a list of her engagements,' he said disappointedly. 'Was the confinement she should have attended this morning at some people called Greenaway, doctor?'

Mortimer nodded.

'It's here.' MacDonald tapped the book. 'There are two other entries after that. Harrington and Jebbworth for this afternoon . . . ' He shook his head. 'I was hoping it might be some sort of a diary,' he said, laying the book down.

'Well, I must be off,' said Doctor Mortimer. 'The Greenaways will be frantic. I only hope the baby hasn't decided to arrive yet.'

He bustled off and they heard the grinding of gears as he drove away.

'We'd better go through the woman's belongings,' said the superintendent, rising to his feet. 'Do you want to stay, Mr. Armitage?'

'I — er — think, if you have no objection,' said the vicar nervously, 'that I should like to remain . . . '

MacDonald offered no objection, and they all three went back to the bedroom. Methodically, MacDonald and Blane went through everything, while the Reverend Colin Armitage looked on with a kind of vague interest. Miss Cheeseman's personal effects were not considerable, but everything was neat and very clean. She had, apparently, been a very tidy woman. The contents of her professional case were in perfect order, but consisted of only those things which a district nurse would be expected to carry.

The other room, which faced the back, was much smaller. It had a few articles of bedroom furniture in it, but was, from the look of it, unused. The bed was covered by a quilt, but had not been made up.

Gradually they worked through the entire house, but they found nothing to reward them for their diligence.

'Well, that's that,' remarked Superintendent MacDonald, when they had finished. 'There's nothing here that's likely to help us.'

Leaving a uniformed constable in charge of the house, he dropped the vicar at the Vicarage, and drove to Midchester. Inquiries would have to be started at once into the past life of the dead woman, in the hope that they would yield some clue to the motive for her death. But MacDonald was not very sanguine.

Although he couldn't accept it as a certainty, at the back of his mind he was convinced that they had to deal with a lunatic.

And that was going to be difficult. Because the kind of lunatic who went about strangling women might be quite normal in every other respect.

Yes, it was going to be difficult.

8

The news of the second murder spread rapidly through Lesser Sweeping, passing from mouth to mouth with the speed of a bush telegraph. It reached the Manor shortly after eleven o'clock, being conveyed thence by the milkman — who told the cook, who informed the butler — and eventually reached Sir Robert.

His usually florid face was pasty and drawn, and he looked as though he had slept badly as he paced up and down the library with knitted brows. The news had shocked him tremendously. There was a big responsibility on his broad shoulders that rested there like a physical weight. What ought he to do? If only he were *sure*, there was only one thing to do . . .

But he *wasn't* sure . . .

All his fears and forebodings might be imaginary. It would be a terrible thing if he took any action and was wrong . . . A terrible thing.

Presently, he left the library and ascended the broad staircase to his brother's room. Hesitating for a moment outside the closed door, he tapped.

His brother's voice called faintly, 'Who is that?'

'It's I — Robert,' he answered.

The door was opened and Richard appeared on the threshold.

'Come in,' he said, and Sir Robert entered, closing the door behind him.

'How are you today, Richard?' he asked.

Richard Stanton passed a trembling hand across his forehead.

'It's my head,' he complained. 'I don't seem to be able to think clearly . . . '

'You should rest more,' said his brother, and his usually dictatorial voice was very gentle. 'You were out last night.'

'Was I?' said Richard dully. 'I don't remember. Sometimes I can remember everything plainly, and then something seems to come over my mind, like a thick blanket . . . '

'I know, I know,' said Sir Robert. 'You have been taking your tablets regularly?'

'Yes, I think so,' answered Richard. 'Yes, I have — of course I have . . . '

'Where did you go last night?' asked his brother.

'Go?' replied Richard, shaking his head. 'I've told you — I don't remember going out . . . Are you sure I went out?'

'I came to your room — just before midnight,' said Sir Robert. 'You were not here. You must give up going out at night, Richard. It's not good for you . . . '

'I like it at night. It's quiet and peaceful,' said Richard. 'People stare at you so in the daylight . . . '

'Why don't you keep to the park?' suggested his brother.

'I suppose I could do that,' said Richard doubtfully, and then, with a sudden note of irritability in his voice, 'Why do you fuss so?'

Sir Robert made a little gesture in which there was a tinge of despair.

'You've been very ill, you know,' he said. 'I don't mean to fuss, as you call it. I'm only trying to do what is best for you.'

'Dear old Bob,' said Richard, his troubled eyes softening. 'I — I'm sorry.

I'm a great trouble to you . . . '

'No, no, old man — never think that,' said Sir Robert, laying his hand on his brother's shoulder. 'Both Harriet and I are very fond of you.'

'Harriet's been a brick,' said Richard. 'If only my head would clear. I don't know what I'm doing sometimes . . . The other day, I found myself in the High Street. Do you know, I had no recollection of going there? It was as though I had been asleep and suddenly woken up.'

There was a deep sadness in Sir Robert's eyes as he looked at the other.

'That's all part of your illness,' he said. 'Doctor Bachause assured me that there would be no recurrence of that . . . '

'I don't like Doctor Bachause,' said Richard. 'I never did like him. He's pompous and stupid. He thinks I'm mad . . . Did you know that? But I'm not . . . I'm not mad . . . '

'No, of course you're not,' declared Sir Robert heartily, but his heart was heavy. 'Well, I must go and write some letters. I'll see you again at luncheon.'

He went downstairs and into the

drawing-room. Lady Stanton was sitting at a writing table in the window, checking the household accounts. She was a plain woman with a rather horsey cast of feature, but with a smile that made up for all her other lack of beauty.

'Harriet,' said Sir Robert abruptly. 'I'm worried.'

She looked up from her perusal of the grocer's book.

'Richard?' she inquired.

'Yes.' He went over to the fireplace and stood with his back to the grate, his favourite position. 'You've heard what happened — to the district nurse?'

She nodded and laid aside her pen. Her rather colourless eyes clouded.

'You're not suggesting . . . ?' she began.

'Nothing,' he broke in. 'I'm not suggesting anything, Harriet. But Richard was out last night. He doesn't remember it, but he was . . . '

'Oh no,' she protested in a low voice. 'No, Robert. That would be terrible . . . '

'We've got to face the possibility, m'dear,' said her husband. 'Richard . . . well, we know that he's not — not mentally stable . . . '

'But he wouldn't . . . It's ridiculous, quite ridiculous,' she said. 'He was never violent . . . '

'You never can tell what sort of turn it might take,' said Sir Robert. 'I suppose I was wrong to take him away from the home. But I thought he was cured . . . '

'Of course you did,' said Lady Stanton. 'We both thought so. So did Doctor Bachause . . . '

'He's still very — ill,' said Sir Robert. 'There's no doubt about that. Keeps complaining about his head. Says he can't get things clear. He's not as bad as he was, but . . . he hasn't entirely recovered.'

She got up and came over to his side, resting her elbow on the mantelpiece.

'What are you going to do?' she asked.

He shook his head uncertainly.

'I don't know,' he declared. 'That's the truth. I don't know what I *ought* to do . . . '

'It would be better to do nothing than to do the wrong thing,' she said.

'That's what I feel.' There was a certain amount of relief in his voice. 'I'm glad you agree. But it's a big responsibility . . . '

'We've got to accept it,' she said.

★ ★ ★

On the day following, the newspapers flaunted the double murder at Lesser Sweeping in leaded type. As a sensation it was enough to gladden the heart of any news editor. The means of murder; the eccentricity of the murderer in sending the key of his victim's house to the vicar of the parish; the fact that that particular vicar happened also to be the well-known crime novelist, Armitage Crane — added up to an almost perfect story. And the newspapers went to town on it!

Lesser Sweeping swarmed with reporters. Everybody even remotely connected with either of the two victims, and a large number of people who were not, were interviewed. The Reverend Colin Armitage was almost driven frantic. Four telephone messages and three telegrams arrived at the Vicarage during the course of the day, each offering him fabulous sums for articles on the crimes.

'Why don't you accept, Daddy?' said Merle, when she saw the amounts that were offered. 'This is real money.'

Her father shook his head.

'It's quite out of the question, my dear,' he said. 'It would not do at all, not in my position.'

'I wish they'd let *me* do it,' said Merle. 'Gosh, think of what I could buy.'

The vicar looked alarmed.

'I must really forbid you to think of such a thing,' he exclaimed. 'I couldn't possibly allow it.'

'I don't suppose anybody will ask me,' said Merle wistfully. But her father wasn't so sure. Failing him they might be prepared to consider an article from the feminine angle from his daughter. He extracted a promise from her that on no account would she do such a thing.

Superintendent MacDonald shut up like a clam at the first advent of the reporters, and refused to make a statement of any kind. He had set inquiries going concerning both Sylvia Shand and Miss Cheeseman, and he was awaiting any reports that might come in. And towards the close of that day he gained an unexpected and useful piece of information.

He had just returned to his office after arranging for the inquests, when a message was brought to him that a woman wished to see him.

'She says she's the sister of Miss Cheeseman, sir,' said the constable who brought the message. 'Come all the way from London, she says . . . '

'Show her in at once,' said MacDonald with alacrity.

The constable departed and a few seconds later returned with a little, stout woman of about fifty. Her round face was troubled and her eyes red with crying.

'Sit down,' said the superintendent kindly, pulling forward a chair. 'You are the sister of Miss Cheeseman?'

'That's right, sir,' answered the little woman. 'Mrs. Hunter, sir. When I read in the newspaper what 'ad happened to Gladys, I come at once . . . '

'I'm very glad you did, Mrs. Hunter,' said MacDonald.

'It don't seem possible that such a

thing could've 'appened to Gladys,' sniffed the other, dabbing at her eyes with a very moist handkerchief. 'Always so bright an' jolly she was, too.'

MacDonald couldn't quite see why that should have prevented her being murdered, but didn't say so.

'I only 'ad a letter from her last week,' continued Mrs. Hunter. 'Full of 'er new job, it was, and how she was settlin' in. She'd seen somebody here she thought she knew, too, an' . . . '

'She'd seen somebody here? Do you mean in Lesser Sweeping?' asked Mac-Donald, breaking in unceremoniously.

'I suppose that's what she meant, sir,' said Mrs. Hunter. 'I've got the letter 'ere, if you'd care to read it.'

She opened her handbag, fumbled about among its contents, and finally produced a letter which she held out to MacDonald. He took it and read the following, written on a sheet of ordinary notepaper, torn from a writing block:

Dear Muriel,
This is just a short line to tell you

that I got that job I told you about and I have been here a week. The house is a nice little house though I shall have to get a bit more furniture when I can afford it. There's a spare bedroom so if you can get down any time to see me you could always stay for a day or two and of course longer if you could manage it. The doctor here is a very nice man but a bit brusque but it is just his way and he doesn't mean it. By the way, do you remember that woman I told you about during the war — the one in the bombed block of flats? Well, I'm sure I saw her here the other afternoon in the High Street. Her hair was different but you know my memory for faces. I'm sure it was the same woman. I wonder if her husband is with her? This is a very short letter but I've got to go off to a call and I will write again soon. Your affectionate sister,

Gladys.

'Who was this woman your sister told you about?' asked the superintendent.

'It was an experience Gladys 'ad during the war,' replied Mrs. Hunter, looking rather surprised at the question. 'One of them doodlebug things, it was. Fell on a block of flats in Kensington. Made a nasty mess of 'em, so Gladys said. She was with the W.V.S. then, you see. Well, this woman and her husband, 'e was on leave or something, was in one of the damaged flats.'

'Miss Cheeseman must have been involved in a good many such 'incidents',' said MacDonald, as she paused for a moment. 'What made her remember this one in particular?'

'I was going to tell you that,' said Mrs. Hunter. 'You see, the woman accused her husband of trying to strangle her . . . '

'Strangle her,' exclaimed the superintendent sharply.

'That's what Gladys said,' answered Mrs. Hunter. 'She made an awful fuss about it, Gladys said. But the husband only laughed and said it was all nonsense. It was the shock of the bomb, he said, that had upset his wife. Gladys said she was in a very hysterical state. But it stuck in her mind, you see . . . '

Superintendent MacDonald felt that he was getting somewhere at last. If the woman Miss Cheeseman had recognised had been Sylvia Shand, here was the link between them. And the husband? His wife had accused him of trying to strangle her during the bomb incident. And both the murders had been strangulations. There was definitely a link here . . .

'Did your sister mention the name of this woman?' he asked.

Mrs. Hunter shook her head.

'No,' she answered. 'I don't know whether she knew it. Funny she should have seen 'er here.'

Was the husband here, too, thought Macdonald, and had he been afraid that the district nurse's 'memory for faces' would result in her recognition of him? Was that the reason for her death? It was a possible theory. It might also account for Sylvia Shand's presence in Lesser Sweeping . . . Apparently, from what Miss Cheeseman had told her sister, this husband had tried to strangle his wife before. Had he succeeded this time? A good many years had elapsed since the bomb incident. What had happened to him in the meanwhile? Had he still been living with his wife before she rented the cottage? There had certainly been no sign of any husband there ... But Miss Cheeseman had believed that the husband 'was on leave or something.' If that were so, then he would have gone back to his regiment. Had he left his wife?

MacDonald made a mental note to have the bomb incident inquired into. Even after all this time it might be possible to get a list of the people who had been living in the block of flats at that period. Somebody else, beside Miss Cheeseman, ought to remember the wife's accusation ...

'Do you know who killed Gladys?' The voice of Mrs. Hunter broke in on his thoughts.

'Not yet,' said MacDonald.

'I 'ope you find him,' said Mrs. Hunter vindictively. 'I'd like to 'ave a go at him with my bare 'ands, I would. Gladys was a good woman. She never did no 'arm to anyone. This other woman was killed in the same way, wasn't she?'

MacDonald admitted that she was.

'There's too much o' this violence going about these days,' said Mrs. Hunter, shaking her head. 'Something ought to be done about it. You can't pick up a paper without reading about something 'orrible happening. What are the police for, that's what I'd like to know.'

'We can't do miracles,' said MacDonald. 'We're doing our best to find this person, you know.'

Mrs. Hunter sniffed.

'And when you do find 'im,' she said, 'they'll want to wrap 'im up in cotton wool an' see that he don't come to any harm. All this rubbish about not 'anging murderers . . . Jest asking for trouble *that* is. What about the people they kill? Nobody ever seems to think about *them*. All they can do is whine about the poor feller what's going to get 'is rightful desserts an' hang. It isn't right.'

The superintendent, privately, was in complete agreement with her. But he had no wish to enter into an argument on the pros and cons of capital punishment.

'Are you staying for any length of

time?' he inquired.

'Well, I thought I'd like to see Gladys buried,' said Mrs. Hunter, not, perhaps, expressing herself too happily. 'And then there's 'er things. Somebody'll have to take charge of them, won't they?' She sniffed and dabbed her eyes with the wispy handkerchief. 'I suppose there'll be an inquest?'

'The day after tomorrow, in the village hall at Lesser Sweeping,' said Mac-Donald. 'You will be able to arrange for the funeral after that.'

'I think I can manage to stay until then,' said Mrs. Hunter, and soon afterwards she took her departure to look for suitable accommodation.

As soon as he was alone, MacDonald put through a long distance call to Scotland Yard. To the detective-inspector he was connected with, he explained carefully and fully what he wanted, and eventually sat back in his chair with the satisfactory knowledge that the inquiries concerning the block of flats, and who had occupied them at the time of the bomb incident, would be put in hand at once.

At least he had a little more to go on now. If it proved that the woman of the flats had been Sylvia Shand, then it seemed that the husband might turn out to be the man they wanted. But he still had to be found. If they could get a good description of him, or were lucky enough to find out his name, then he might be traced through his war service up to a certain point. It wouldn't be so easy after that. But still, it was something to go on — more than there had been yesterday. Perhaps tomorrow would bring to light something more . . .

He sighed.

That was detective work. Adding a little piece here and another little piece there. Nothing sensational or exciting — just sheer hard work and a great deal of thinking.

He didn't know it, but the excitement and sensation were yet to come.

9

'You know, Betty,' remarked Mr. Payne, at breakfast on the following day, 'this place is getting impossible — absolutely. I dithered out for a spot of the old fresh air, oxygen, ozone, and all that, and got hijacked by a bally swarm of reporters.'

Elizabeth Payne laughed.

'What did you do?' she asked.

'What *could* a fellow do?' demanded her husband with his mouth full of bacon and egg. 'They jolly well wanted some news so I duly obliged. By jove, they were frightfully grateful.'

They were having breakfast in Elizabeth Payne's bedroom. They usually had it here, since she was not allowed to get up too early. The woman, who came in every morning to cook and clean, laid two trays — Elizabeth only had tea and toast — but it was Payne who insisted on carrying them up to his wife's room, and also on having breakfast with her.

'What on earth did you tell them?' she asked. 'I didn't think you knew anything.'

'I didn't,' he answered calmly. 'But I made up a jolly good story — absolutely top-hole. Remembered a bit out of a book I'd read.'

'Ronnie,' exclaimed his wife. '*What* did you tell them?'

'All about the man I'd seen creeping through a wood a week before that woman, Shand, was killed. Absolutely first-class stuff. Sent cold shivers down my spine . . . '

'You'll get into trouble,' she interrupted anxiously.

He shook his head, and swallowed a huge portion of toast.

'Don't you worry the old grey matter,' he declared. 'I couldn't disappoint 'em, poor chaps. They were frightfully keen to get hold of something. I told 'em that this fellow in the wood had a white face and great staring eyes and that he was dressed all in black. I said that he was crouching like a hunchback, and that he was muttering to himself. They swallowed it all, like little Tommy at the jam cupboard.

It was jolly good, really. Good mind to try my hand at whiffling off a few thrillers. These chaps make fortunes out of 'em. Look at old Armitage . . . '

'He writes wonderful books,' said Elizabeth.

Her husband looked a little doubtful.

'Do you really think so?' he said. 'Too deep for me. I can't get the hang of 'em. All those times and alibis. Absolutely beats me. I prefer something with a bit more go in it. Like old what's-his-name who wrote thingummyjig.'

'In fact,' said his wife, 'you're thoroughly enjoying all the excitement of these murders, aren't you?'

Ronald Payne looked a little sheepish.

'Well,' he confessed, 'it does break up the old monotony a bit. Like Worcester sauce with cold mutton, if you know what I mean.'

For a moment her eyes clouded.

'It must be very dull for you, dear, married to an invalid like me,' she said.

'Oh, here, hold on, old thing,' cried Mr. Payne. 'I didn't mean that, you know . . . '

'I know you didn't mean it,' she said,

'but it's true, all the same . . . '

'It's not true at all,' said her husband indignantly. 'You couldn't jolly well be dull if you tried, old top. Full of the good old whatnot — absolutely brimming over with it . . . '

Laughter chased away the momentary cloud from her eyes. It was that queer, dithering, incoherent way of talking that always made her laugh. It was strange, she thought, but it was just that that had first attracted her to Ronnie. She knew that a lot of it was put on for her benefit — for the express purpose of making her laugh. But a great deal of it was a natural characteristic, all the same, and it had set him apart from the more serious men whom she had met. He refused to treat life as anything but a huge joke, and although this might have irritated some women, it suited her.

'I think I'll stagger along to the village and see if I can pick up any news,' he said, lighting a cigarette. 'If I run into any more reporters, I shall have to tell 'em my classic story of the bloodstains on the gate.'

'Don't be silly, Ronnie,' she said seriously. 'You'll only get yourself into trouble . . . '

'You can trust me, old darling,' he said, bending down and kissing her. 'I'm the most wonderful trouble dodger you ever met. Trouble takes one good look at me and beats it down the next turning.'

He waved to her from the door and went downstairs. Putting a rose in his buttonhole as he walked through the garden, he let himself out by the side gate and sauntered in the direction of the village.

It was a beautiful morning with every prospect of another hot day ahead, and Ronald Payne whistled softly as he turned into the lane that led down to the High Street. The first call he made was at the tobacconist's to buy some cigarettes.

The little shop was run by an elderly woman named Mrs. Grimp. She looked like a witch and had the reputation among the children of actually being one. This she had carefully fostered because it had the effect of stopping any suggestion of cheekiness on the part of her small customers. They were too afraid of the consequences to be rude to Mrs. Grimp.

'Good morning, Mr. Payne,' said this formidable-looking woman, emerging from behind a pile of sweet bottles as he entered the shop. 'It's a powerful nice day.'

Ronnie agreed that it was. He asked for a hundred cigarettes of his favourite brand.

'How is Mrs. Payne?' inquired Mrs. Grimp, as she found a box and wrapped it up.

'She's about the same,' he answered. 'Bearing up, you know. Keeping the old flag flying, and all that.'

'Ah,' said Mrs. Grimp, shaking her head. 'It does seem that some is burdened with affliction that don't deserve it.' She looked so hard at Ronnie as she said this, that he wondered if *he* was the special affliction that she imagined Elizabeth Payne to be burdened by.

'Such things that are happening these days,' went on Mrs. Grimp. 'Battle, murder, and sudden death, it seems 'as overtaken us.'

'Oh, I say, you know,' expostulated Mr. Payne, 'that's rather putting it strongly, eh? No sign of any battle, what?'

'Ah,' said Mrs. Grimp darkly. 'There's no saying what's in store for us. Wonderful are the ways of Providence.'

Mr. Payne could think of no suitable reply to this, so he paid for his cigarettes and drifted out of the shop. On the pavement he almost ran into Michael Ferrall.

'Hello, Ronnie, you're out early,' greeted Ferrall.

'Just pottering around, old boy,' answered Mr. Payne vaguely. 'Though I might pick up a few unconsidered trifles, eh?'

'You'll probably pick up plenty,' said Ferrall. 'There are all sorts of rumours flying about if, of course, you are referring to the murders?'

'Well, of course I am,' said Mr. Payne. 'Betty's simply seething with curiosity. Got to try and find some news to tell her. Cheers her up no end, you know. Have you heard anything?'

Ferrall shook his head.

'It's my opinion there's a lunatic about,' said Mr. Payne, looking over his shoulder as though he expected to see the lunatic bearing down upon them. 'That's the jolly old solution, old boy, you'll see.'

Rather to his surprise, Ferrall seemed disturbed.

'I wouldn't go spreading that round, if I were you,' he said.

'Why not?' inquired Mr. Payne, raising his eyebrows. 'Seems to me a pretty sound idea, eh? I mean to say, here's a chappie going round strangling females ad lib. Why? Can't be just because he doesn't like their faces, you know . . . '

'He might have a very good reason,' said Ferrall.

Mr. Payne looked unconvinced.

'Can't be any good reason, old boy,' he said. 'Just a kink, like thinking you're a poached egg. You know — belfry full of bats, top story to let, doolally, dotty . . . ' He tapped his forehead.

'I gather what you mean,' said Ferrall dryly. 'But I think there's more to it than that. I suppose you'll be coming to the inquest?'

'Oh, rather,' said Mr. Payne. 'Betty'll want all the gen. When is it, old boy?'

'Tomorrow morning — in the village hall,' said Ferrall. 'Well, I must be pushing off. Got some business to attend to.'

'Drop in for a spot this afternoon?' invited Mr. Payne. 'Always pleased to welcome old friends, eh? Have a noggin at the ancestral home . . . '

Ferrall said he would if he could, and hurried away. Mr. Payne continued his aimless way down the High Street. He met a number of people whom he knew, and discovered that the sole topic of conversation was the murders. He was considering returning home by a different route when he ran into the vicar. It would be more literally true to say that the vicar ran into him.

The Reverend Colin Armitage was walking rapidly along as though in a dream, and bumped into Payne before he even saw him.

'I beg your pardon,' he said, peering in surprise at the other. 'Dear me, I really wasn't looking where I was going . . . '

'Working out a new murder?' said Payne cheerfully.

'A new murder?' repeated the vicar

doubtfully. 'Oh, I see what you mean . . . No, no, I was thinking about these terrible tragedies that have occurred in our midst. Shocking! There is a very callous and wicked man at work, I fear.'

Mr. Payne advanced his theory of a lunatic.

'Possibly, possibly,' said the vicar, without any marked conviction. 'At the same time, I don't exactly agree. It seems to me . . . ' He broke off suddenly. 'Oh, excuse me, there is my daughter, I think, looking for me.'

Merle came quickly across the street.

'Really, Daddy, you're incorrigible,' she said severely. 'What do you mean by running away like that?'

'Running away?' said the vicar, regarding her with mild surprise. 'I don't understand, my dear . . . '

'You came into the stationer's to buy some paper,' said Merle. 'I left you for a moment to look at some pencils, and the next minute you'd disappeared.'

'Good gracious, yes — paper,' said the Reverend Colin Armitage. 'That's extremely important, my dear. I have very nearly run out of paper . . . '

'Then why didn't you get it?' demanded his daughter.

'I was under the impression that I had,' said the vicar. 'Dear me, how extraordinary. I was quite *sure* that I had . . . '

Mr. Payne chuckled.

'Done the same thing myself, old — er — padre,' he said. 'The old brain-box goes off on another tack, so to speak, eh? Fearfully upsetting. I remember popping down once to the farm to get a chicken. Got thinking of something else and popped back. No chicken. Had to fake up something for dinner that night, eh? Betty frightfully annoyed . . . '

'I'm not surprised,' said Merle. 'Both you and Daddy should have a keeper. We'd better go back and get the paper . . . '

The vicar agreed obediently and trotted off by the side of his daughter, leaving Mr. Payne, rather amused, staring after them.

Wonderful, he thought, how the old codger turned out those books of his. You'd never imagine that he had sufficient intelligence.

He took a road back home that led along a bridle path into the woods. As he walked slowly under the overhanging trees, he saw a figure approaching him from the opposite direction. It was the figure of a man, and he was striding rapidly along the twisting path, his head down, and his long arms swinging at his sides.

It was Richard Stanton!

He didn't notice Ronald Payne until he was almost facing him and then he looked up, startled.

'Good morning,' said Payne. 'Absolutely wonderful day, eh?'

Stanton muttered something, and hurried on. Payne frowned. The man's face had been white and drawn and his hands were clenching and unclenching convulsively as he walked. He turned to look back. Richard Stanton was gesticulating violently as though he were warding off unseen enemies.

Odd, thought Payne, as he continued on his way, very odd. The man was definitely queer. What was the matter with him?

He thought of the story he had told the reporters that morning and smiled. It hadn't been so far from the truth, actually. He *had* seen a man in the woods, and the description he had given might very easily apply to Richard Stanton.

10

The inquest on the following morning was a matter of extreme disappointment to the reporters present and to those residents of Lesser Sweeping who had hoped for sensation.

There was nothing sensational about it at all.

Evidence of identification, and the medical evidence regarding the cause of death, was taken and then, at the request of Superintendent MacDonald, the coroner adjourned the inquiry pending further evidence. The entire proceedings were over in under an hour.

'Absolute washout,' said Payne to Ferrall. 'No lurid details of any sort. Jolly tame, eh? Betty'll be fearfully disappointed.'

He looked at the little woman in black who had identified the body as that of her sister. Mrs. Hunter, with the wisp of handkerchief still very much to the fore, was talking to Inspector Blane.

'Looks frightfully cut up, eh?' he said. 'Not very nice for her, old boy.'

'Worse for her sister,' said Ferrall curtly.

'I say, by the way,' continued Payne. 'What's up with Richard Stanton, eh?'

'What do you mean?' asked Ferrall sharply.

'Saw him yesterday morning, old boy,' said Payne. 'Met him as I was going home through the woods. Something definitely queer there, eh? I mean, did he get a touch of the sun or something in Africa?'

'There's nothing the matter with him at all,' said Ferrall.

'Oh, I say, come now, old boy,' protested Payne. 'You ought to have seen him. Face all white and sort of twitching, and his eyes looked like burnt holes in a sheet. Sort of understudy for Dracula, absolutely. Gave me a scare, I can tell you . . .'

'He — he suffers a bit from nerves — that's all,' said Ferrall.

'By jove, I should think he did,' exclaimed Payne. 'If I had nerves like that, old boy, I'd jolly well do something about it . . . '

'I've no doubt the family are looking after him adequately,' said Ferrall shortly. 'It's none of your business, or mine.'

'All right, all right,' said Payne. 'No need to get all stuffy and upstage, eh? Only telling you what I saw . . . '

'What *did* you see, Mr. Payne?' the voice of Superintendent MacDonald broke in. He had come up behind them and overheard the latter part of what Payne had been saying. 'Anything more about this mysterious man in the woods?'

Ronald Payne looked guilty.

'Well, you know,' he said, 'I — er — Look here, did those reporter chaps tell you?'

'It was in the papers,' said MacDonald. 'Why didn't you tell me about it before? You never mentioned it when I called to see you after the death of Sylvia Shand.'

'I hadn't thought of . . . ' Payne broke off in confusion.

'You hadn't thought of it then, is that what you were going to say?' asked the superintendent sternly.

'Well, er — as a matter of fact you're absolutely bang on,' said Payne. 'You see, it was like this, old chap . . . ' He explained the situation.

'I see,' said MacDonald. 'Then you didn't actually see this man at all? It was only a story for the benefit of the reporters?'

'That's right,' said Payne. 'I jolly well had to say something. Fearfully persistent lot of beggars, these chaps. Sort of waylaid me, you know. Absolutely . . . '

'Well, I should advise you not to make up any more stories,' said MacDonald. 'You'll find yourself in trouble if you do.' He nodded curtly and moved away.

Ronald Payne took out his handkerchief and mopped his face.

'I say,' he said, 'that was a bit of a spot.'

'He gave you very good advice,' said Ferrall. 'I'll give you some more. Just forget all this nonsense about Richard Stanton.'

'But that was absolutely the truth, old boy,' began Payne.

'I said forget it,' cut in Ferrall, and he walked away.

Payne shook his head a little disconsolately.

'Always falling in the old consommé,' he muttered, and drifted off to seek solace in a pink gin at the local pub.

Superintendent MacDonald went back to Midchester as soon as the inquest was over. Although he believed that the solution for the two murders lay in the bomb incident recounted by Gladys Cheeseman to her sister, he couldn't afford to neglect everything else. There was always the possibility that the attempted strangling episode had been a coincidence. It was what a man in a temper might easily do — take his wife by the throat without any serious intention of actually throttling her. It had to be taken into consideration, anyhow. In the meanwhile, there was Sir Robert Stanton and his brother. There was something wrong there. Both of them had been afraid of something.

Richard Stanton was supposed to have recently come back from South Africa, but he hadn't looked like a man who had been in a tropical country. He looked like a man who had been ill — in hospital . . .

MacDonald thought that it was definitely worth looking into. Doctor Mortimer had said that he *was* ill. Was it a physical illness, or — mental . . . ?

Now, here was a possibility . . .

Supposing that he *was* mental, could he have homicidal tendencies? The superintendent shook his head. He was going a bit too far without any evidence to warrant it. Because a man looked ill, you couldn't attribute murder to him — not without undeniable facts to bolster such a theory up. But that period of absence would have to be inquired into. If he *had* been in South Africa, as was generally supposed, there should be some proof of the fact. If he hadn't . . . Well, then somebody must be able to prove where he *had* been.

Sir Robert Stanton?

It would not be a pleasant interview but it would have to be faced. Might as well get it over and done with . . .

MacDonald had his lunch and drove back to Lesser Sweeping. On his way past the vicarage to pick up Inspector Blane, he thought he'd call in on the vicar. He was quite a clever old bird. He might be able to help. He wanted to tell him about the dead woman's story to her sister, anyway.

The Reverend Colin Armitage was in his study and welcomed the superintendent in his usual courtly manner.

'I hope that this unexpected visit means that you have brought some news?' he said, leaning back in his chair behind the untidy desk.

'Well, yes, sir,' said MacDonald, and he proceeded to recount the arrival of Mrs. Hunter, the letter she had received from her sister, and the story of the bomb incident.

The vicar listened with intense interest.

'Dear me,' he remarked, when the superintendent had concluded, 'this is of the utmost importance. We now have a definite link between the two dead women . . . '

'If Sylvia Shand was the woman Miss Cheeseman thought she recognised,' said the superintendent. 'That hasn't been definitely established.'

The vicar picked up his glasses and

swung them gently between his fingers.

'I — er — I think you are being a little too cautious,' he said. 'Both these women were strangled, and obviously by the same person — the receipt of the key by me in both instances proves that. I think, at least as a working hypothesis, we are justified in concluding that Sylvia Shand and the — er — woman in the flat were one and the same person. If we accept that, it opens up some very interesting possibilities.'

'You mean with regard to the husband, sir,' said MacDonald.

The vicar nodded.

'Yes, yes, of course,' he answered. 'The husband would appear to be the — er — most likely candidate for our unknown murderer.' He pursed his lips thoughtfully. 'That leads us to a very interesting question,' he continued after a slight pause. 'Did Sylvia Shand come to Lesser Sweeping to avoid this man, or did she come to seek him?'

MacDonald nodded. It was a question he had asked himself.

'It seems to me that she came to seek

him,' he said. 'If he were not *still* in the district there would have been no motive for the murder of the district nurse . . . '

'You mean,' said the vicar quickly, 'that he killed her because he was afraid that she might recognise him as the husband in the episode of the bombed flat?'

'Exactly,' agreed the superintendent. 'Which seems to suggest, sir, that he is, and has been, living somewhere in the neighbourhood.'

'That is very sound reasoning,' said the Reverend Colin Armitage. 'It leads, of course, to the further question: what was his — er — wife's reason for seeking him out?'

'To which there could be several answers, sir,' said MacDonald. 'She may have still been in love with him; she may have been trying to get money out of him for her support; she may have wished to marry again and wanted a divorce; a dozen reasons . . . '

'None of the ones you have mentioned seem to me strong enough to warrant murder,' said the vicar doubtfully.

'You'd be surprised at the number of

murders that have been committed for a totally inadequate reason, sir,' said the superintendent.

The Reverend Colin Armitage smiled.

'I don't think I should,' he answered. 'I've made rather a — er — study of murder, you know.'

'In connection with your writing,' said MacDonald.

'Yes. There are several main motives for murder,' the vicar continued. 'Gain, which is the commonest; safety, which comes next; jealousy, fairly common; revenge, which is rather rare in this country; and to retain respectability, which really comes under the heading of safety. We know so little at present that it is difficult to suggest under which category the first of these murders should come. The second is, without much doubt, I think, a murder for safety. Miss Cheeseman was killed because the murderer was afraid of her . . . '

'Always supposing, sir,' said MacDonald, 'that we are dealing with a logical motive.'

The vicar nodded slowly.

'Yes,' he said. 'And against that supposition you have the murderer's action in forwarding me the keys of his victims' habitations. In any logical explanation you would have to include a logical reason for that . . . '

'But not if the murderer was not responsible for his actions, sir,' said MacDonald.

The Reverend Colin Armitage tried to rub his forehead, found that rather to his surprise he couldn't manage it, and discovered that he still held his glasses in his hand. He put them on, and blinked at MacDonald.

'You — er — you have some reason for that possible conclusion?' he asked.

'Yes, I'm thinking of Mr. Richard Stanton,' said the superintendent, and he proceeded to explain what was in his mind.

'I see.' The vicar removed his glasses, looked at them with a puzzled expression, as though he wondered what on earth they could be, and put them down on his blotting pad. 'There may be something in what you say. My — er — daughter, Merle, was saying that she thought there was something definitely wrong with

Richard Stanton, and Doctor Mortimer was inclined to think the same . . . Dear me, though, it's very puzzling . . . Surely it would be too much of a coincidence to suppose that he should have chosen Miss — er — Cheeseman for his second victim?'

'Coincidences *do* happen, sir,' said MacDonald.

'Yes, yes, of course, undoubtedly,' agreed the vicar, 'but . . . perhaps I am looking at it with the novelist's mind . . . but . . . ' His voice trailed away and he shook his head.

'Whichever way you look at it, sir,' said MacDonald, 'you come up against a snag. If you try for a logical solution, you are faced with the *illogical* action of the keys. If you adopt the maniac theory, you come up against a thundering coincidence . . . '

'So we must be looking at it the *wrong* way,' said the vicar. 'The true explanation should completely discount coincidences and illogicalities . . . '

'That isn't always possible in real life, sir,' said the superintendent.

'It's possible more often than you

might believe,' said the Reverend Colin Armitage. 'In the present case, I think, we are trying to construct a hypothesis without sufficient data. That is the root of the difficulty. For instance, we are assuming that Sylvia Shand is the woman referred to in Miss Cheeseman's letter. I'll admit that we have a very good reason for assuming that, but it is not a certainty. Next, we are assuming that the husband mentioned in the story Miss Cheeseman told her sister, is still alive. That, again, is not a certainty. Then, we are assuming that Richard Stanton is suffering from some form of mental complaint . . . '

'That can easily be settled, sir,' said MacDonald.

'But it cannot so easily be settled as to what form it takes,' argued the vicar. 'There are a number of mental illnesses that are quite harmless, except to the unfortunate sufferer. Has Richard Stanton shown any signs of homicidal tendencies before?'

'That is my reason for seeing Sir Robert,' said MacDonald. 'I am convinced, from my own observation, that they're both afraid of something . . . '

'You know your own business best, superintendent,' said the vicar, 'but I should strongly advise you to wait . . . '

'It's too dangerous,' said the superintendent. 'If Richard Stanton is at the bottom of this business — mind you I don't say he is, but *if* he is — there's no knowing when he'll strike again. We don't want a third murder . . . '

A very worried expression came into the vicar's eyes. He stroked his brows as though the action might soothe away the trouble on his mind.

'No,' he said soberly. 'We don't want a third murder . . . '

11

Sergeant Pickering, of the Criminal Investigation Department, New Scotland Yard, very quickly discovered that his assignment regarding the people who had lived in the block of flats in Kensington, at the time the doodlebug had fallen on it, was going to be difficult.

To start with, the building had been very severely damaged, and the greater portion of its inhabitants had left soon after the bomb had devastated their homes for less dangerous localities. Several families, then occupying the flats, were dead; an equal number untraceable.

The damaged portion of the building had been rebuilt, but the people living there, at the time he began his inquiries, were mostly new tenants. He discovered two who had been living there at the period he was interested in, an elderly couple and a spinster lady. Unfortunately, they couldn't supply him with any information concerning the woman and her husband, who had occupied one of the lesser damaged flats, and they failed to recognise the photograph, taken after her death, of Sylvia Shand.

If he had been able to supply the number of the flat, it might have helped, but this he couldn't do. He went to the estate agents who had had the letting of the flats at that time, but they couldn't help him either. He tried the shops in the immediate neighbourhood, and at a small tobacconist's, kept by an old man who possessed the shrewdest pair of eyes that Pickering remembered seeing in anybody's face, he got his first piece of luck.

'I remember the doodlebug falling,' he said. 'It was in the early days of 'em. Among one of the first to fall on London, it was. I was younger then, o' course, an' I went over to see if I could 'elp. I think I remember the young woman you're askin' about. She used to be a customer o' mine. That was in the days when it was difficult to get a packet o' cigarettes unless you was a regular customer . . .'

'This is a photograph of the woman,'

said Pickering. 'Can you see any resemblance to the woman you're talking about?'

The old man took the photograph and carried it under a light. Very carefully he gazed at it, and then slowly shook his head.

'Seems like it might be,' he said, 'but I couldn't say for certain. The young woman I thought it might be when you asked me, had a bit of a mole under her chin, but you can't see anythin' of the sort in this here photograph.'

'A mole under the chin, eh?' said Pickering. 'Whereabouts exactly?'

The old shopkeeper pointed to the photograph.

'Just there,' he said.

The sergeant made a note of the position.

'Did the woman you're talking about have a husband?' he asked.

'I don't know whether 'e was 'er husband or not,' answered the old man with a chuckle. 'You couldn't tell in those days, could yer? But she 'ad a man with her sometimes when she come in for her cigarettes.'

'What was he like?' asked Pickering.

The old man shrugged his shoulders.

'Now you're askin' something,' he said. 'There wasn't much difference between 'em then, was there? 'E was in uniform, o' course.'

'What uniform?' inquired Pickering.

'I can't tell you that,' said the old man. 'It wasn't the R.A.F., that's all I can say.'

'Do you know what this woman's name was?' asked the sergeant.

'No,' said the other.

'Didn't her husband call her anything?' said Pickering.

Again the old man chuckled.

'I expect he called 'er a lot o' things, if it were 'er husband,' he said, 'but I never 'eard him call 'er anything. I'll tell you who might be able to 'elp you, though,' he added, as a sudden thought struck him. 'The ladies' 'airdresser's, across the street. The woman I'm talking about used to go there.'

Sergeant Pickering thanked him.

The receptionist at the desk in the hairdresser's was a middle-aged woman who listened in surprise to what he had to say.

'We used to have a lot of clients from

146

the flats,' she said. 'I was here at the time they was bombed, just taken on the job, as a matter of fact, but I don't know whether I can help you . . . '

'Here's a photograph of the woman I'm inquiring about,' said Pickering, producing his photograph again. 'It's not a very good one, but where I've made that little pencil tick, just hidden under the chin, she had a mole . . . '

'A mole?' exclaimed the woman quickly. 'That sounds like Mrs. Hemming . . . ' She took the photograph and examined it, frowning. 'Yes,' she said, 'I'm almost sure it's Mrs. Hemming . . . '

Elation ran through Sergeant Pickering's veins. That visit to the old tobacconist's had been a stroke of luck.

'Do you remember,' he asked, 'whether Mrs. Hemming's husband was in the Army?'

'I believe he was,' answered the receptionist. 'I remember a man in uniform calling for her once . . . '

'I suppose it's too much to expect that you can remember what regiment?' asked Pickering.

She smiled.

'As a matter of fact, I can,' she answered to his surpise. 'It was the R.A.M.C. I remember, because I had a boyfriend in the same, at the time. That was just a war-time romance,' she added with a grimace.

Pickering made a note in his book.

'How long was Mrs. Hemming living here?' he asked.

'Well, I couldn't say that,' answered the receptionist. 'She was a client with us for about eighteen months. She may have been here before that.' She hesitated. 'Why are you making these inquiries?' she asked curiously.

'I am just trying to trace her from that time,' answered Pickering cautiously. 'Did she leave soon after the bomb fell?'

'I think so,' said the woman. 'She came in to have her hair done and said it would be the last time as she was going away.'

'She didn't say where?' asked the sergeant.

The receptionist shook her head.

'No,' she replied. 'I didn't like her, you know. None of us did. She was rather shrill and — and overbearing. She wasn't what you would call a lady . . . '

'What was her husband like?' asked Pickering.

'He seemed a quiet sort of fellow,' she answered. 'I only saw him once, if that was her husband . . . '

Pickering asked a few more questions, but he had extracted all the information she had to offer. He left with a feeling that he had been very lucky indeed.

Going back to the Yard, he reported to his immediate superior, who, in turn, got in touch with the Army authorities and put out an inquiry concerning the history of Hemming, who had been in the R.A.M.C. Since there would, without doubt, be a number of 'Hemmings' in the records of the R.A.M.C., he gave as much information about this particular one as he could, the address at the block of flats in Kensington being the most important. The Army authorities promised to do their best, but stated that it would take a little time, and with this Detective-Inspector Meacham had to be content.

He telephoned through to Midchester with the information that Sergeant

Pickering had already acquired, particularly mentioning the mole on Mrs. Hemming's chin.

'That,' said MacDonald, when he received the message, 'clinches the identification. I remember the mole on the dead woman's chin. Mrs. Hemming and Sylvia Shand were one and the same woman.'

After a little thought, the superintendent had decided to take the Reverend Colin Armitage's advice and postpone his interview with Sir Robert Stanton. But he was taking no risks. He stationed a man near the Manor with instructions to follow Richard Stanton wherever he went. The man was to be relieved at stated intervals so that a constant watch was kept day and night.

That, thought MacDonald, would take care of Richard Stanton.

It did, but not quite in the way he had expected.

* * *

There arrived in Midchester on the afternoon of the following day, a rather

150

extraordinary-looking man who inquired the way to the police station and, when he eventually reached it, asked for an interview with the officer 'who was in charge of the Shand business.'

The bearded stranger, who was dressed in shabby corduroy trousers and a bright magenta shirt, with sandals on his otherwise bare feet, was conducted to the presence of Superintendent MacDonald.

The first sight of the stranger reminded MacDonald of the description Ronald Payne had given of the men in the pub. This was definitely art with a capital 'A.'

'I've been thinking the matter over,' said the bearded stranger without preliminary, 'and I've come to the conclusion that I ought to tell the police of something that I know.'

'What's your name?' asked the superintendent.

The other hesitated.

'I don't want to get mixed up in this,' he said. 'I mean, I don't want my name mentioned . . . '

'I can't promise anything,' said the superintendent. 'It rather depends on what you have to tell me . . . '

'It's nothing to do with me,' said the bearded man, hastily. 'It's only something I saw when I was staying at Sylvia's cottage here. I shouldn't have come forward about it, only — well, it's been worrying me . . . '

'I'm afraid we must have your name,' said the superintendent.

'It's Plush,' said the bearded man. 'Horace Plush . . . '

MacDonald wrote it down, feeling that if he had a name like that he wouldn't want it known, either.

'Well, now, Mr. Plush,' he said, when he had added the man's address, 'what is it you have to tell me?'

'Some weeks before — er — well, before it happened,' said Mr. Plush, 'I, and some friends of mine, were staying at the cottage for a week-end. Sylvia was fairly generous with the liquor and we'd all been drinking a good bit. We weren't drunk, but it wouldn't have taken much more to make us paralytic. Somebody, one of the girls, I think, asked Sylvia where she got all the money from to live like she did. Good food and tons of drink and things. Sylvia laughed and said that it was none of our business. During the night, I got infernally thirsty. I'd drunk all the water in my room and I got up, put on my dressing-gown, and went downstairs to get some water from the kitchen tap. There was a light in the sitting-room and naturally I looked in. I thought somebody had gone to bed and left the light on. But Sylvia was still up, or she'd got up, and she was putting something away under the carpet. I said: 'Hello, what are you doing? Playing hunt the thimble?'

'She was a bit startled, rather frightened, I thought, but when she saw it was me, she laughed. She'd been drinking pretty heavily — I thought she'd probably been at it after we'd all gone to bed — anyway, she said: 'That's where the money comes from, Horry.' I said: 'Good lor', don't tell me you keep a private cache under the carpet?' She shook her head. 'There's no money there,' she said. 'Look, see for yourself, if you don't believe me.'

'She hadn't put the carpet back, and when I came closer, I saw that there was a little square opening in the floor, like a box. There was nothing in it but a folded paper. 'That's worth a lot of money to me,' she said, 'and it's going to be worth even more one of these days.' She kicked the lid of the box shut and pulled the carpet over it. 'You needn't go shouting about that all over the house, either,' she said. 'I was a fool to tell you.' She pushed me out of the room in a sudden rage and slammed the door. I got my water and went back to bed. That's all there is, but I thought it might have something to do with the murder, and I ought to tell you.'

'I'm very much obliged to you, Mr. Plush,' said MacDonald. 'It was very good of you to come forward with this important information. Could you suggest what this paper might have been?'

The bearded man shook his head.

'No,' he said. 'I didn't really have time to see it properly. She kicked the thing shut too quickly.'

MacDonald looked at his watch.

'It won't take very long to run over to the cottage,' he said. 'I'd be glad if you would come with me and show me this place where you saw the paper.'

Mr. Plush was a little reluctant, but he agreed. The superintendent sent for a car, collected the keys of the cottage from his desk, and they set off.

The cottage looked very pretty and peaceful in the sun, with its surrounding masses of roses. It was almost impossible to believe that violence in any form had taken place there. Superintendent MacDonald unlocked the front door and they entered the hall. There was a stuffy smell permeating the closed house, and the sweet and rather sickly odour of old perfumes.

They went into the sitting-room, and the superintendent turned back the carpet.

'Here, was it?' he asked, and Mr. Plush nodded.

'A little further back,' he said. 'Yes, there you are.'

He pointed to where one of the floor boards had been sawn through and hinged. It had been done by an amateur, the workmanship was crude, and as a hiding place it wasn't very original. MacDonald took out his penknife and prised open the lid.

The cavity beneath was empty.

'Nothing there now,' he said.

'That's where it was,' said Mr. Plush.

MacDonald pushed down the lid and pulled the carpet back into place.

'Either it was taken by the murderer, or the dead woman herself moved it to a safer place,' remarked the superintendent. 'Probably she regretted having shown you the hiding place.'

MacDonald locked up the cottage again, drove Mr. Plush back to the railway station at Midchester in time to catch his train to London, and went back to his office.

Gradually, it seemed, he was acquiring a little more information about the dead woman. What was the paper which was so valuable and was likely to be even more so in the future? A will? It rather smacked of blackmail. Was that the motive for the woman's death? With the exception of the original five hundred pounds which had opened the account, there had been no large sums of money paid into her bank. But that did not preclude the possibility of blackmail. She might have lodged the money elsewhere. Perhaps she was clever enough to believe that large sums in cash paid into her account would have looked suspicious and, of course, the person she was blackmailing wouldn't have paid by cheque. More than likely she'd opened a post office account in another name . . .

In the midst of his conjectures the telephone rang. It was the Reverend Colin Armitage.

'I've been — er — pondering over this business,' said the vicar. 'There's something I'd very much like you to do for me, if it wouldn't be too difficult.'

'What is it you want, sir?' asked MacDonald.

'It's in reference to those keys,' replied the vicar. 'In case there should — er — be a third key . . . '

'Good Heavens,' exclaimed the startled superintendent. 'You're not expecting that, are you?'

'I don't think we ought to take it for granted that there won't be,' said the

Reverend Colin Armitage mildly. 'That's why I wish to offer this suggestion. I hope you won't think that I am trying to usurp your own — er — '

'No, no, that's all right, sir,' broke in MacDonald. 'What is this suggesion of yours?'

'I imagine it should be possible to get in touch with the postal authorities and — er — arrange for the man who collects the letters from the village to telephone either you or me, should there be a small parcel among the collection . . . '

'By James, that's a good idea sir,' said MacDonald.

'I thought it was worth doing,' said the vicar modestly. 'You see, the parcel is small enough to go in the post-box and it would be addressed to me — I think we can take that as certain. Now, in the last instance, the — er — murderer posted the key of his victim's house to catch the last collection in the village, which meant that he posted it *before* he committed the crime . . . '

'If we had had the key when the post was *collected* instead of waiting for it to be *delivered*,' interrupted MacDonald, 'we should have been in possession of it before the murder . . . '

'Exactly,' said the vicar. 'So that, presuming we could identify the key, we should be in a position to prevent a further crime.'

'I'll attend to it at once, sir,' said the superintendent.

'The very greatest secrecy must be observed,' said the vicar. 'It must not be allowed to — er — leak out to anyone . . . '

'I'll arrange about that, sir,' said MacDonald. 'It's a very good idea, though I'm afraid it's rather like locking the stable door after the horse has gone . . . '

'I wouldn't be too sure of that, superintendent,' said the Reverend Colin Armitage, and he rang off.

159

12

Michael Ferrall came to the end of the bridle path and struck off across a narrow track that would take him back to the Manor. He had been to inspect some property belonging to the Stanton estate. It was an old farmhouse and cottages that required a great deal of repair. Ferrall was tired. Although he was related to the Stantons he worked hard for his living. The job of steward was no sinecure.

It was a beautiful afternoon. There seemed no sign of the heat-wave breaking. The sun shone on field and wood and meadow from a cloudless sky, reflecting yellows and green in all shades and striking a tinge of red from tiled roofs. But Ferrall was not taking a lot of notice of the beauties of nature that lay all around him. His brow was furrowed and the expression of his eyes was troubled.

He came to the end of the track and

160

turned sharply into a twisting path that skirted the woods. Following this would bring him to a gate which led into the grounds of the Manor. It was here where Ronald Payne had encountered Richard Stanton. The path led to the Paynes' house too, but in the opposite direction.

Ferrall paused to wipe the sweat from his forehead. He was only wearing slacks and an open-necked shirt but he was very hot. He saw someone coming along the path and presently recognised Richard Stanton. His cousin was moving in his usual jerky fashion, his head bent forward, his eyes on the ground.

Ferrall had no wish to run into him just then. He left the path and took to the shelter of the trees. They grew thickly close up to the winding track, and he was soon hidden among their trunks. After Richard had gone by, he would continue on his way home.

Looking neither to right nor left, Richard Stanton drew nearer. Ferrall could see the drawn, haunted look on his face, and the spasmodic movements of his hands, with their long, curling fingers.

The man looked as though he were on vibrating wires . . .

Ferrall watched him until he had passed by, and he was in the act of returning to the path when he saw a second man strolling slowly along in Richard's wake.

He was a thin man in a darkish suit, and he moderated his pace so as to keep the same distance between himself and the figure of the man in front.

He was obviously following Richard, and, as he came abreast of where Ferrall was concealed among the trees, and he got a clearer view of him, there was no mistaking what he was.

He was a detective!

So the police were interested in Richard Stanton, were they? That was going to upset Sir Robert and Harriet. They had been worried enough, but this was going to put the climax on it . . .

He'd have to tell them. It was no good keeping it dark. Robert would have to do something about it. In Ferrall's opinion the best thing he could do was to go straight to Superintendent MacDonald and make a clean breast of the whole thing.

It had been a mistake, right back at the start, to try and hush the thing up — a bigger mistake to have ever brought Richard back. Doctor Bachause had said that he was cured, but was there any certainty of a cure in these cases?

Richard Stanton had shown tendencies of being mentally unbalanced ever since he'd been a child. Nothing very serious, just fits of depression and bad temper which had grown steadily worse. As a boy in his teens he had refused to mix with other boys of his own age but gone off on his own for long solitary rambles. And he was queer in many ways, moody and flying off into passions of senseless rage.

But the Stantons hadn't called in a specialist. It was not until a few years ago that they'd done that, after there was no doubt that Richard was growing steadily worse. Ferrall supposed that they'd hoped he'd grow out of it. For long periods at a time he would be very nearly normal — never quite, but sufficient to pass muster. He'd never been so bad as he was now . . .

After one of his bad fits, Robert had

called in Doctor Bachause. He had come as an ordinary friend to stay for the weekend and from the signs he had observed, he had diagnosed Richard as being insane. But he held out hopes of a complete cure. It would mean a prolonged course of treatment in a special clinic. Richard was persuaded to go, and it was given out that he had gone to South Africa . . .

Of course, the taint was in the family. Robert and Richard's great-grandfather had died as batty as a coot . . . and *his* grandmother before him . . . That's what made the whole thing so worrying — you never knew . . . It might pop up in you, or worse, in your own children. The family blood was in your own veins . . .

Ferrall sighed. If it wasn't for that possibility — that lurking doubt — he would long ago have asked Merle Armitage to marry him. He had known her since she was a child and had gradually become aware of her attractiveness . . . Oh, well, that was impossible. There'd probably be an open scandal, now the police had got on to Richard, and the whole thing would come out . . .

Superintendent MacDonald must have found out somehow about Richard and, of course, suspected him of the murders. It was only natural. He didn't think, himself, that Richard had had anything to do with strangling those women, but there was always the chance that he might have in one of his fits of mind-blankness. But it was unlikely that he would have sent those keys to the vicar . . . Still, you couldn't blame the police for being suspicious and taking precautions.

What would Sir Robert do when he told him? There wasn't much he could do, but he'd be very upset — so would Harriet. It wasn't very pleasant to have a thing like that in the family — not a proud family like the Stantons . . .

Near the gate leading into the park he almost ran into Merle. She had just come out of the wood where she had been collecting ferns.

'Mother likes them for the vases,' she said. 'They look so nice as a background to flowers. We don't see much of you these days, Michael.'

'I'm usually pretty busy,' he answered. 'I don't get much time.'

Merle made a grimace.

'Surely you could spare a minute to come and see your old friends,' she said. 'You *do* look a bit worried,' she added, eyeing him critically. 'What's the matter?'

'Nothing very much,' he replied lightly. 'There's quite a lot to do looking after the estate, you know. Always something that wants repairing or renewing . . .'

For a moment he almost felt like telling her the truth, but it wasn't entirely his secret.

'Why not walk back with me to the vicarage and have some tea?' she suggested. 'Or are you *too* busy?'

The very slight suggestion of malice in her tone decided him. After all, that could do no harm . . .

'I'd like to,' he said. 'We can take a short cut through the park . . .'

Mrs. Armitage was very pleased to see him.

'Why, Michael,' she said, 'this *is* nice. It must be ages since we've seen you. Linda's laying tea on the lawn — or I

166

hope she is,' she added. 'I did tell her to, but you never can tell . . . '

'She is, mother,' said Merle. 'We saw her as we came in. Where's Daddy? In the study?'

'Well, he wasn't a few minutes ago,' said Mrs. Armitage. 'I went to tell him that tea would be ready, and the room was empty. I don't know *where* he is . . . '

Merle laughed.

'I expect he'll turn up after it's all over,' she said. 'I'll go and put these ferns in water. Would you like a wash, Michael? You look a bit sticky.'

'I would, as a matter of fact,' he said.

'You can find your way to the bathroom, can't you?' said Merle. 'You ought to — it's still where it used to be.'

It was another gentle little dig at his long absence, and Michael flushed slightly. She had a right to be a little resentful, he thought. They had been almost inseparable companions in the old days — before he had known of the taint that lay over his family. Merle, and he and Tommy Pritchet . . . He had been a little jealous of Tommy, he remembered, but

167

Tommy had married and left the village . . .

He washed his hands and sluiced his face and went down again feeling cooler and fresher.

Mrs. Armitage was pouring tea when he arrived, but there was no sign of the vicar.

'This is quite like old times, Michael,' said Mrs. Armitage, handing him a cup of tea, as he sat down in a basket chair. 'Help yourself to bread and butter. There are strawberry and gooseberry jams — I remember you always liked gooseberry — and some of those cakes you used to be so fond of . . . '

'We couldn't get rid of him at one time, could we, mother?' said Merle, nibbling at a cake.

'Michael was always welcome here and always will be,' said Mrs. Armitage. 'Good gracious, how the time does fly. Why it only seems like yesterday that you two were children . . . '

'I sometimes wish those days were back again,' said Michael Ferrall. 'I know, I seem to have dropped off coming to see you all, but there really has been a good reason for it . . . '

'Such a *very* busy man,' said Merle with an exaggerated note of awe in her voice.

'Well, I have got *quite* a lot to do,' he said.

'I'm sure you must have,' said Mrs. Armitage. 'But you mustn't overdo it, you know. All work and no play is not good for anyone.' She looked round as Linda came up with a jug of hot water. 'Linda, has the vicar come in yet?'

'Did 'e go out?' asked the untidy Linda, setting the jug down with a bang that slopped part of its contents over the cloth.

'Oh, do be careful, Linda,' said Mrs. Armitage. 'He must have gone out. He's not in the house anywhere . . . '

'Well, 'e ain't come in then,' said Linda, and she wandered back to the house, revealing a large hole in the heel of one of her black stockings.

'I can't think *where* he can have gone,' said Mrs. Armitage, shaking her head.

'He probably hasn't the least idea

himself,' said Merle. 'You know what Daddy's like.'

'Indeed I do, my dear,' said her mother with feeling. 'Perhaps he's gone to the church for something, or he might have gone down to the post office for some stamps. That is one of the things he's always forgetting . . . '

'It's not much use trying to conjecture where he's gone,' said Merle. 'You'd probably be wrong, anyway. Daddy is completely unpredictable . . . '

By no stretch of the imagination could they have predicted where the Reverend Colin Armitage was at that moment, or what he was doing.

13

The Reverend Colin Armitage, in the middle of the nineteenth chapter of his new book — a particularly tricky one in which a clue to the murderer's identity, while being perfectly fair, had to be presented in such a cunning way that the reader would not be able to spot it — suddenly felt the urgent need of fresh air.

Laying down his pen — he wrote all his novels in this old-fashioned way, eschewing the typewriter or tape recorder — he went over to the French window that opened into the garden, and walked out.

Still thinking over the difficult passage in chapter nineteen, he went on walking, oblivious to the fact that he had passed out of the gate and was making his way along a narrow lane that would eventually bring him to the woods.

It was not until he was actually among the trees that he became conscious of his surroundings. Looking up with mild surprise, he paused and frowned. There were no trees like these in the vicarage garden. What was he doing here? He had strolled out of his study for a breath of fresh air ... A few minutes, that was all ...

He looked at his watch.

It was nearly five o'clock. He remembered that it was only a quarter past four when he had risen from his writing table ...

Really, he must have been walking for nearly three-quarters of an hour without the faintest idea of the passing of time or where he was going. Well, at least he'd got that tricky part of chapter nineteen clear. That's how it could be done, he thought — quite simple. Writing these stories was really rather the same technique as a conjuror inventing a new trick. The art of misdirection. That was it, in a nutshell. You took care to fix the reader's attention on something that didn't really matter while you slipped the real thing, that did, in casually.

He'd have to hurry back or he'd miss his tea, and he suddenly discovered that he was thirsty. He was making his way out from amid the trees when he stumbled over something, and very nearly went sprawling. A fallen trunk . . . ?

No, it had been too yielding for that, too soft . . .

He stooped, adjusting his glasses . . .

It was the body of a man!

'Dear me,' said the Reverend Colin Armitage.

The man was thin-faced and dressed in a suit of some dark grey material. He had obviously not been laying there for any length of time. His clothes were quite clean and so were his boots. The vicar stared at his boots. Regulations boots . . . ?

Dropping on to one knee, the vicar tried to discover what was the matter with the man. He thought at first that he might have been overcome by the heat, but he quickly found out his mistake. The man was dead! And the apparent cause of death was — strangulation!

Armitage rose slowly to his feet and looked about him. It was absolutely still, here, at the fringe of the wood. He could hear an occasional bird flutter in the leaves above his head, but that was all.

The stillness of a hot summer afternoon hung over the entire countryside.

'Dear me,' remarked the Reverend Colin Armitage again, and pondered what he should do next. He couldn't stay here. He would have to get help. This was another murder. It flashed through his mind that this time the murderer couldn't send him a key. There are no keys to woods. The body must be seen by the police as soon as possible. The best thing he could do would be to seek out Inspector Blane. He could then get in touch with Superintendent MacDonald . . .

At a little, jerky trot, the vicar set off by the nearest possible route to the village. Breathless from his unwonted exercise, he arrived just as the inspector was sitting down to his tea. But Blane forgot all about his tea when he heard what the vicar had to tell him.

'I believe it's one of our men, sir,' he said. 'Sounds like it from your description. I'll get on to the super.'

He was only just in time to catch him, for MacDonald was on the point of going out.

'I'll be over at once,' he said. 'Who found him? The vicar? Keep him with you until I get there.'

He rang off. Before leaving Midchester, he put through a call to the Manor, and asked if Mr. Richard Stanton was at home. The call was put through to Sir Robert, who demanded to know who he was.

'This is Superintendent MacDonald speaking. Something very serious has happened, and it is imperative that I should know whether your brother, Mr. Richard Stanton, is at home.'

'He isn't,' said Sir Robert, and there was anxiety in his voice. 'What's the matter? Has anything happened to him . . . ?'

'I shall be coming to see you shortly,' said MacDonald, cutting in. 'I'll tell you then.'

He looked very grave when he arrived at Lesser Sweeping.

'I don't think there's much doubt that the dead man is Detective-Constable Hollings,' he said. 'And I've less doubt that Richard Stanton killed him. This is what comes of listening to your advice, vicar,' he added reproachfully.

The vicar looked astonished.

'My advice?' he repeated.

'You asked me to hold my hand over Richard Stanton,' said MacDonald. 'I did, but I arranged to have him followed wherever he went. Hollings was on duty this afternoon . . . '

The Reverend Colin Armitage looked troubled.

'I should be very sorry to think that any advice of mine should have led to such a serious result,' he began.

'It was mostly my fault, sir,' said MacDonald. 'I shouldn't have listened to you. I'd like to see exactly where you found the body. I've already arranged for the police doctor and the rest to pick us up here . . . '

They arrived ten minutes later, and then they all set off for the place where the vicar had found the body.

The body had not been disturbed. It still lay just as he had first seen it.

'That's Hollings,' said MacDonald tersely, looking down at the still form that lay amid the tangled undergrowth.

'Getting to be an epidemic, this

strangling business,' grunted the doctor, as he knelt down and began a swift examination. 'H'm . . . He was strangled, but he was knocked out first. See this wound on the back of the head? Made with a jagged stone or something similar . . . It didn't cause his death. See that thin cord sunk in the flesh of the neck? Same as the other two, eh?'

'Aye,' said MacDonald grimly. 'There's little doubt now who the killer is. We'll pull in Richard Stanton at once . . . '

'I suppose you are quite sure?' said the vicar.

'Aren't you, sir?' said the superintendent. 'This cord clinches the matter, in my opinion. It's the same method as the others . . . '

'Yes, yes,' agreed the vicar. 'There can be no doubt that this man was killed by the same person who murdered Sylvia Shand and Miss Cheeseman, but was that person Richard Stanton?'

'You need a great deal of convincing,' said MacDonald.

The Reverend Colin Armitage rubbed his forehead.

'It is too serious a matter to take anything for granted,' he replied.

'Well, I don't know what more you want, sir,' said the superintendent. 'Hollings was following Stanton when he was killed. There's no reason why anyone else should have done it . . . '

'No — no, I suppose not,' said the vicar doubtfully. 'But I cannot reconcile Richard Stanton with the sending of the keys to me . . . '

'A man with a kink is likely to do all kinds of things,' said MacDonald. 'Richard Stanton's insane, in my opinion, and not responsible for his actions. Sir Robert will have quite a lot of explaining to do,' he added. 'He must have been aware of his brother's state . . . '

'You are going to the Manor?' asked the vicar.

'As soon as we've finished here, sir,' said MacDonald. 'It's no good your suggesting, this time, that I shouldn't . . . '

'I wasn't going to,' interrupted the vicar. 'I was only going to ask if you would object to my coming with you?'

MacDonald hesitated.

'I don't see what good that will do, sir,' he said.

'I should be very grateful if you would agree,' said the vicar.

'Very well,' said the superintendent grudgingly.

The Reverend Colin Armitage said no more but stood waiting in the background until the routine attaching to a murder inquiry had been attended to. When the photographers and fingerprint men had done their job, and a constable had been left to guard the body, pending the arrival of the ambulance to take it to the mortuary, he joined MacDonald in the police car with Inspector Blane, and they drove to the Manor.

They were shown into the library and after a brief delay Sir Robert came in. His face was clouded with anxiety and he looked almost haggard.

'What has happened?' he demanded without preliminary. 'Your telephone message worried me greatly, superintendent . . .'

'Aye, it needs to,' said MacDonald curtly. 'There's been another murder.'

'Another — murder?' repeated Sir

Robert, and his voice was suddenly so hoarse that it was scarcely audible. 'Who . . . ?'

'One of my men,' said MacDonald. He related briefly and tersely what had happened. 'Where is Mr. Richard Stanton?' he asked.

'He hasn't returned,' said Sir Robert. 'I feel sure there must be some mistake . . . '

'I don't think there's any mistake, sir,' said MacDonald. 'I should like you to tell me the truth about your brother, Sir Robert.'

'The truth — I don't know what you mean . . . ' Sir Robert tried to regain something of his usual dignity, but it was a feeble attempt.

'I think you do, sir,' said the superintendent sternly. 'I should warn you that this is too serious a matter for any more hushing up.'

'If I may give a word of advice, Stanton,' said the vicar. 'I think Superintendent MacDonald is right. No good can come of further dissembling. It will not help Richard . . . '

Sir Robert walked over to the window

and stared out into the sunlit garden. After a moment he turned and he seemed to have aged several years, so furrowed was his brow and so lined his face.

'Very well,' he said harshly and jerkily. 'I'll tell you — the truth.'

He told them. He told them of Richard's boyhood and the first signs of the taint and of the steps he had taken.

'You should have reported this to the police, sir,' said MacDonald, when he had finished. 'You must have realised that there was a strong possibility that Richard Stanton was responsible for the death of Sylvia Shand . . . '

'God help me, I didn't know what to do,' exclaimed Sir Robert. 'I was afraid — yes, I'll admit that I was afraid Richard might have had something to do with it, but I wasn't sure. How could I be sure? And, after all, he was my brother . . . '

'I can appreciate that, sir,' said MacDonald. 'But, if you had come forward then, these other murders might have been prevented.'

'I can't believe — I can't believe, even now, that it *could* be Richard,' cried Sir

181

Robert. 'If I had had any proof . . . '

'I'm afraid that I shall have to take immediate action,' said the superintendent.

'Does that mean . . . does that mean that you intend to — to arrest my brother?' asked Sir Robert.

'I'm afraid it does, sir,' said MacDonald.

'There is always the possibility that he will be proved innocent,' said the vicar.

'Why do you say that?' asked Sir Robert. 'Do you *believe* that?'

'I am not entirely convinced of his guilt,' answered the vicar cautiously.

'You hear that?' said Sir Robert, turning to MacDonald. 'That's how I feel about it . . . '

'Aye,' said the superintendent, nodding. 'I hear what the vicar says, but I shouldn't be doing my duty if I took any notice of it. If he could produce any proof of Richard Stanton's innocence it would be a different matter . . . '

'Did you adopt that suggestion of mine?' inquired the vicar.

'Suggestion, sir?' For the moment MacDonald was not quite sure what he meant, then it came to him. 'There's no need to go on with that arrangement now . . . '

'Oh, please, continue it,' said the Reverend Colin Armitage earnestly. 'I consider that it is very important — very important indeed.'

MacDonald shrugged his shoulders.

'Well, I don't mind leaving the arrangement as it is, just to please you, sir,' he said. 'But it seems a little futile now . . . '

'If there *should* happen to be — another,' said the vicar, 'while Richard Stanton was — er — under arrest, that would prove his innocence, would it not?'

'It would go a long way,' agreed the superintendent, 'but there won't be.'

'Another what?' asked Sir Robert looking from one to the other in surprise. 'What are you talking about? Another murder?'

'No,' said the vicar. 'Only the prelude to one . . . '

14

Richard Stanton did not come back to the Manor that night. Superintendent MacDonald waited until a fairly late hour and then, leaving Inspector Blane — to that worthy man's obvious discomfiture — to await the arrival of the wanted man, he went back to Midchester to have an 'all stations' call put out for the apprehension of Stanton.

What small element of doubt that had remained in his mind concerning Richard Stanton's guilt, a doubt engendered by the vicar's attitude, was now completely dispersed by his disappearance. However, he was pretty confident that the missing man would not remain missing for long. Stanton's appearance and general demeanour were so very much out of the ordinary that with every policeman in the country on the lookout for him, it was only a matter of hours before he would be brought in.

There was a report from Scotland Yard

awaiting him when he got back, but it was not until the following morning that he opened it. By this time, he was getting definitely uneasy about Stanton. There had been no news of him at all. Of course, he might be wandering about in the woods surrounding Lesser Sweeping, in which case it could be days before he was found. They were many, and thick, and a man could hide himself for a considerable period until hunger forced him to seek food.

Although MacDonald thought the report concerning Mrs. Hemming's husband was now of little interest to him, he was a conscientious man and so he read it while he awaited news of, so he thought, more importance.

The War Office had succeeded in tracing Hemming. He had been an orderly in the R.A.M.C. His full name was James Gregory Hemming. He had married in the early days of the war, apparently, for when he originally joined up no marriage allowance appeared on his papers. This had been added in nineteen forty-two, when a marriage allowance was made to Dorothy Hemming, of Fourteen Greyland Court,

South Kensington. Hemming had a medium record. He had several times been punished for overstaying his leave. That seemed to have been his principal offence. None of this mattered very much, thought MacDonald, when he came to the end of the report. '*This man was killed in France on 'D' day.*'

So that was that!

Hemming was out of the case.

By four o'clock that afternoon, when there was still no news of Richard Stanton, MacDonald went over to the vicarage. He had promised to let the vicar know the full result of his inquiries concerning Sylvia Shand and, as yet, he hadn't been able to. He thought he might put that straight and perhaps at the same time score a small triumph.

The vicar was in his study, grappling with his new book, but he appeared to be only too pleased to lay it aside and welcome the superintendent. He was evidently surprised when MacDonald informed him that there was still no news of Richard Stanton.

'Dear me,' he said, 'that's very strange

186

— very strange. I don't like it, you know — I don't like it at all. What can have happened to him?'

'I expect he's hiding up somewhere,' said MacDonald. 'We're bound to get him eventually. It's only a question of time. I've got some information about Sylvia Shand. I thought it would interest you.'

'Indeed it does,' said the Reverend Colin Armitage. 'What have you found out about her?'

'Her real name was Dorothy Hemming and she was married to a man in the R.A.M.C. — an orderly. They were married in nineteen forty-two and lived at that block of flats that was damaged by the bomb — Greyland Court.' He paused.

'Well?' prompted the vicar. 'What happened to the husband?'

'The husband,' said MacDonald, 'whose name, by the way, was James Gregory Hemming, is dead. He was killed in France on 'D' day.'

'Was he indeed?' remarked the vicar, frowning. 'Dear me, that's very annoying. It upsets my theory . . . '

'It doesn't upset mine, sir,' said MacDonald.

'No, no, it wouldn't,' said the Reverend Colin Armitage. 'You are so sure of Richard Stanton being the guilty man, are you not? So this man, Hemming, is dead? Very, very disappointing. H'm ... I suppose there's no doubt of that?'

'That's what the report from the War Office states, sir,' said the superintendent.

'There have been mistakes made, even by the War Office,' remarked the vicar. 'H'm ... well, is that all you have to tell me?'

'That's all, sir,' said MacDonald, and then as he suddenly remembered: 'Oh, aye, there was one other thing. One of the dead woman's — Mrs. Hemming — one of her friends came to see me ... ' He related the story that the bearded Mr. Plush had told him, and what they had found when they went to the cottage.

The vicar was intensely interested. He asked several questions concerning Mr. Plush, his appearance, where he lived, and whether the superintendent had checked on the address.

'Well, as a matter of fact, sir, I didn't,' answered MacDonald, rather surprised.

'There seemed to be no need to. The man came forward of his own accord . . . '

'Yes, yes, possibly you're right,' said the vicar. 'Dear me, this is very interesting — very interesting indeed . . . '

'Considering what's happened,' said the superintendent, 'it doesn't seem of much importance . . . '

'Not much importance?' echoed the vicar. 'Good gracious me! It is of the *first* importance. Don't you realise that this almost confirms my opinion that Richard Stanton is *not* the person who murdered these people?'

'It doesn't affect mine, sir,' said MacDonald.

'Then it should,' retorted the vicar. 'You should never allow a preconceived theory to blind you to the facts. You are deliberately refusing to take notice of those facts that point to Richard Stanton's innocence.'

'What are they?' asked the superintendent.

'They are these,' answered the vicar, leaning forward and resting his elbows on his blotting pad. 'First: the keys. Second:

this paper which was seen by Mr. Plush, and the remarks made by the woman about it. Third: the choice of Miss Cheeseman as the second victim. You can't reconcile those with the actions of a homicidal maniac, which I presume, you are crediting Richard Stanton with being? You can't provide him with any reasonable motive.'

'What about the murder of Hollings, sir?' said MacDonald. 'Was there a reasonable motive for that?'

'Yes, indeed,' said the vicar. 'I think I could suggest a very reasonable and diabolical motive for that . . . '

'Which would also include the disappearance of Stanton, sir?' said the superintendent.

'Yes.' The Reverend Colin Armitage got up from his chair and walked over to the window. 'MacDonald,' he said after a slight pause, 'I've been thinking a great deal over this — er — business. I had evolved a kind of skeleton theory. It was very hazy and lacking in any kind of confirmation. But each fresh fact that you have discovered has fitted it. Therefore, I believe it to be more than partially correct. It does not include a homicidal maniac, but a very cunning and clever man . . . '

'Who?' demanded MacDonald bluntly.

The vicar shook his head.

'I can't say,' he answered. 'I have a vague suspicion, but it seems absurd and far-fetched. If, however, you continue with the postal arrangements, as suggested, I think there is a good chance of catching this man in the act . . . '

'Do you mean, sir,' exclaimed the astonished superintendent, 'that you believe this man is planning a *further* murder?'

The vicar nodded, and his expression was very solemn.

'Yes,' he said. 'I am quite sure of it. He *has* to, if my theory is correct.'

In spite of himself, MacDonald was impressed.

'Can't you give me any hint as to who it is, sir?' he asked.

'I'm afraid I can't,' said the vicar. 'Just in case I should be wrong, it would be grossly unfair. I can only suggest to you that you shouldn't consider the War Office infallible . . . '

'You mean that Hemming is still alive, sir?'

'I'm sure he is,' declared the Reverend Colin Armitage. 'What I don't know is what he is calling himself these days.'

A shadow darkened the sunlight outside the window and Michael Ferrall came in. He was looking worried and anxious.

'Hope you didn't mind my disturbing you,' he began.

'Come in, come in,' said the vicar. 'You never used to bother to apologise. I suppose you've come to see if there is any news of Richard, eh?'

Ferrall nodded.

'There isn't, sir,' said MacDonald. 'Not at present.'

'We're all very worried about him,' said Ferrall. 'Where can he be? He must have food . . .'

'I suppose,' said the superintendent, 'that he knows the district round here very well?'

'He should do,' answered Ferrall. 'He's lived here practically all his life.'

'I suppose that would also apply to you,

sir?' said MacDonald.

'What exactly do you mean by that?' demanded Ferrall frowning.

'Only that you may possibly know of a likely hiding place,' said MacDonald.

'Look here,' exclaimed Ferrall hotly, 'are you suggesting that *I* have anything to do with concealing my cousin?'

'I'll be quite candid with you, sir,' replied the superintendent. 'Richard Stanton is a conspicuous man in more ways than one. As you said just now, he must have food. I think that in some way he is getting it. I'm not saying that you are supplying him with it, but I'm pretty sure *somebody* is, or he would have been caught before this. If they are, they're doing a very serious thing. It's not likely to help Richard Stanton in the long run, but the person or persons concerned could get into serious trouble . . . '

Ferrall smiled.

'Thanks for the warning,' he said, 'but it doesn't apply to me or to anyone I know.'

MacDonald took his leave and a few seconds after he had gone, Merle came in. She was surprised to see Ferrall.

'Well,' she said, 'you again! This must be getting to be a habit. We're just going to have tea . . . '

'I can't stop,' he said. 'I only popped in . . . '

'You haven't been asked yet,' broke in Merle.

The vicar smiled.

'Surely Michael doesn't need to be asked, after all these years,' he said. 'We used almost to — er — take him for granted . . . '

' 'Used' is the operative word,' said Merle. 'We all used to do a lot of things that we don't do now . . . '

'I must be getting back,' said Michael Ferrall abruptly. 'In case there is any news of Richard. Both Robert and Harriet are very worried.'

Merle became instantly contrite.

'I'm sorry, Michael,' she said. 'I forgot about Richard.'

'There's no need to apologise,' said Ferrall. 'I know I'm to blame. If you knew the reason why I gave up coming here, you'd understand better . . . '

'What is the reason?' she asked.

He shook his head.

'I can't tell you that,' he said. 'Bye, bye . . . '

He walked quickly out the open window and was gone. Merle looked after him, wrinkling up her nose in puzzlement.

'I wonder what he meant?' she said. 'What do you think is the matter with Michael, Daddy?'

'Have you had any kind of quarrel with him?' asked the vicar.

'No,' she answered. 'He just gave up coming here, that's all. He says he's very busy, but, of course, there's more to it than that.'

'You're very fond of Michael, aren't you, my dear?' said her father gently.

'Yes,' she answered candidly. 'I always have been. That's why it's rather hurtful — being suddenly dropped . . . '

'I think that Michael is very fond of you, Merle,' said the vicar. 'In fact, I'm quite sure he is. The reason he stopped coming was a very good one — or he thought it was.'

'Do you know what it is?' she asked in surprise.

'I think I might be able to guess,' he replied. He shook his head and sighed. 'The sins of the fathers . . . Dear me, I wonder if that can be it . . . ?'

She went over to him.

'What do you mean?' she said. 'The sins of the fathers . . . ?'

'I was thinking of old Sir Rupert Stanton,' murmured the vicar.

'He was the one that was gaga, wasn't he?' said Merle.

'He died hopelessly insane,' said the vicar. 'The present Sir Robert's great-grandfather . . . '

'But what's that got to do with Michael?' demanded Merle, and then, as she saw the expression in her father's eyes: 'You don't mean that — that Michael thinks he's — he's insane . . . '

'No,' answered the vicar gently. 'But I think he's afraid — desperately afraid — that the family taint might come out in his children . . . '

'But Michael's got nothing to do with *that* side of the family,' she said. 'He isn't even a first cousin . . . '

'I should say that his fears are without foundation,' said the vicar. 'But they are probably very real to him. I can understand his attitude and I rather honour it . . . '

'Well, I think it's just downright silly,' cried Merle.

'You see,' said her father, 'he's had the experience of Richard, unfortunately. That hasn't tended to help matters for him.'

'Can't you do something?' she said. 'Couldn't you talk to him and tell him how silly he is?'

'Does it mean a great deal to you, my dear?' he asked.

'Well, yes, it does,' she said. There was no embarrassment in the way she spoke. She and her father had always been friends in the really true sense of the word. She had been used to telling him all her troubles from when she was a child with the absolute certainty that he would understand and help, if he could. 'You see,' she went on, 'I, somehow, have always expected to marry Michael. We used to talk about it as children. I took it for granted . . . '

'And I think Michael did too,' said the vicar. 'I'll do what I can, my dear.'

She gave him a sudden hug and kissed him.

'Dear old Daddy,' she said affectionately. 'You don't know how much I love you . . . '

Mrs. Armitage appeared at the window.

'Aren't *either* of you coming to tea?' she demanded plaintively. 'Really, Merle, you're getting as bad as your father.'

15

'What train are you catching, dear?' asked Mrs. Payne, after dinner that evening.

Her husband looked up from his coffee.

'Good lor',' he ejaculated, 'I'd forgotten all about it, absolutely, old darling . . . '

She laughed.

'Really, Ronnie,' she said. 'You know that you arranged a fortnight ago to go up to London and see Mr. Lines . . . '

'You mean, you did,' he answered with a grin, looking at her over the rim of his cup. 'I jolly well hate going up to London, fumes and traffic choking you and butting you all over the place. Can't I leave it for another month? Heat wave and all that at the moment, old dear . . . '

'I'm afraid you can't leave it, Ronnie,' she said. 'Mr. Lines wants those papers I signed. They're rather important . . . '

'Post 'em,' interrupted her husband. 'Wonderful invention, the post office.

Bung a letter in the box and, hey presto, Birmingham, Leeds, Manchester, and what-not, the next morning. No trouble. All done by kindness.'

'This has got to be a personal matter,' said his wife. 'I'd go myself, if I could . . . '

'Sorry, old thing,' broke in Payne contritely. 'Don't worry. I'll don the city man's armour — bowler hat, striped pants, black jacket — and risk getting a heat stroke. What time does the jolly old train leave Midchester?'

'The one you usually catch is the ten forty-five, isn't it?' she said. 'I do feel sorry, having to ask you to go, Ronnie, but it's really important . . . '

'Say no more, my child,' exclaimed Mr. Payne. 'I go on the wings of the wind, absolutely. Change at Egglesfield and Nontrotten!'

'You are ridiculous,' said Elizabeth Payne, looking at him affectionately.

'There's gratitude,' said her husband. 'I have just arranged to face the danger of being roasted alive in a hot and stuffy train — unless, of course, we have snow during the night, in which case it will be freezing alive — and all I get in the way of thanks is being called ridiculous.'

He put down his empty coffee cup and, going over to her, kissed her lightly on the top of the head. She put up her thin hand and caught his fingers.

'I think you're very sweet,' she said.

'Danger of diabetes?' he said. 'Overdose of sugar content in the blood. That's me, absolutely. The original glucose phenomenon! Born with a stick of barley sugar in his mouth. I say,' he became suddenly serious, 'I don't like leaving you here all alone . . . '

'Why not?' she said in surprise. 'You've done it before . . . '

'Ah,' he answered, 'there were no homicidal maniacs in the land in those days . . . '

'They'll probably have caught Richard Stanton by then,' she said. 'You know, Ronnie, it's remarkable that he should have remained at large for so long. How can he? He must be terribly hungry by now . . . '

'And he can't be fed by the ravens, like

jolly old what's-his-name was in the thingummyjig, eh? That's what stirs up the old grey matter, old darling. 'Man cannot live on bread alone,' eh? True enough, but man can't live without even bread. Truer still. *Ergo:* Bread must be being supplied. Stands to reason, absolutely.'

'Well, it's rather a roundabout way of putting it,' she said, 'but I see what you mean. Somebody is giving him food?'

He nodded.

'Got it in one,' he said. 'Blood thicker than water and all that, eh?'

'You think Sir Robert is hiding his brother?' she asked.

'Seems pretty obvious,' he replied. 'Kind of hits the old optic bang on, eh?'

'Well, yes,' she said thoughtfully, 'I suppose it does. He couldn't have dodged all those policemen on his own, could he? Poor man, I can't help feeling sorry for him.'

'Oh, look here, old girl,' said her husband, 'he's jolly well killed three people . . . '

'But he didn't know what he was

doing,' she answered.

'Most likely not,' said Mr. Payne, 'but the result's the same, you know, absolutely.'

Elizabeth Payne leaned back in her chair.

'It must be terrible to lose your mind,' she said. 'Far worse than anything physical . . . '

'Never had any to lose, old darling,' said the irrepressible Mr. Payne, 'so I can't say.'

'Don't you ever take anything seriously?' she asked with a smile.

He shook his head.

'Not often,' he replied. 'I'm the clown in the circus. I provide the light relief to the drama of life. I'm the life and soul of the party. 'Laugh and the world laughs with you, weep and you weep alone.' Lot of truth in these old sayings, eh?'

He looked at his watch.

'Time for bye-byes, Betty,' he said. 'You've been up longer today than you ought . . . '

'I feel better, Ronnie,' she said.

'I know,' he answered, 'but you don't

want to overdo it, old dear. You know what Doctor Mortimer said. Plenty of rest, eh? Trot up the wooden hill, as they used to say, and I'll bring you your Ovaltine.'

'You're a good nurse,' she remarked as she got up from her chair. For a moment she hesitated, swaying a little. He was by her side in an instant, his arm supporting her.

'I'm — I'm all right,' she murmured faintly.

'Take it easy,' he said gently. 'Dizzy?'

She nodded.

'A — a little . . . It's going off . . . ' she said breathlessly. He could feel the jerky hammering of her heart. 'I'll be . . . quite all right in a moment . . . '

'I'll help you up the stairs, old darling,' he said. 'Hang on to me and go slowly . . . '

'It's so . . . stupid,' she complained, annoyed with herself. 'If only I could get well . . . like other women . . . '

She would never do that, he thought. He said, lightly:

'I don't want you like other women.

You stay like yourself, by jove, yes, absolutely . . . '

He helped her slowly and carefully up the stairs, pausing frequently so that she could recover her breath, led her into her bedroom and assisted her to undress.

When she was comfortably tucked up in bed, he fetched a glass of water from the bathroom.

'Take your tablet, old poppet,' he said. 'I'll go and make the Ovaltine.'

When he had gone, she lay back among the pillows and closed her eyes. One day, she thought, she would have one of these attacks and she wouldn't recover her breath. The blackness that obscured her sight would grow darker until she sank into it — for ever. It might not happen for years, it might happen next week . . . There was nothing that could be done. The specialists who had seen her had shaken their heads gravely. Rest, no excitement, no worry . . .

Well, she had all that. Ronnie looked after her like a nurse and more. His chatter kept her amused, but she would have given all she had for just two years of perfect health . . . It wasn't much good being rich, if you couldn't do anything . . .

Ronnie Payne came back with the Ovaltine.

'Now, old dear,' he said. 'You just swallow the old potion, and go to sleep . . . '

Later that night, he peeped into the bedroom. She was sleeping quietly and peacefully . . .

The morning dawned with every prospect of another hot day in store. Mr. Payne carried up the trays and breakfasted with his wife as usual. He had not carried out his threat to dress in conventional city attire. Instead, he had put on a light grey flannel suit, with a blue shirt and a dark blue tie. After breakfast, and armed with the documents which were the reason for his journey, he kissed his wife goodbye, took out the car, and drove to Midchester. There was ten minutes to spare before the train left, and he bought himself some cigarettes, a paper and a magazine.

There were not many people on the train and he managed to find a first-class compartment to himself. He was feeling a little worried about Betty . . .

Superintendent MacDonald was feeling worried too, but for a different reason. There was still no news of Richard Stanton. The man might have vanished from the face of the earth, and MacDonald couldn't understand it. Where could he be concealing himself? The chief constable would be asking questions soon, if he wasn't found. It was almost a miracle that a man like Stanton should have been able to remain at large — unless somebody was assisting him? MacDonald's lips compressed. Was that the explanation? Had the man in some way succeeded in getting back to the Manor? That seemed the only explanation. He would have found sanctuary there. His brother wouldn't have given him up. He'd have hidden him and looked after him . . .

The more the superintendent thought about it, the more certain he became that this must be the explanation. There was nobody else in the district to whom Richard Stanton could have gone for help. Well, it could soon be proved, one way or another. He would have to search the Manor. If Sir Robert put up any objection, he'd have to get a warrant. It was unpleasant, but it had to be done.

At half-past eleven that morning, he arrived at the house, accompanied by a very reluctant Inspector Blane. Inspector Blane had been born in the district and to him the people of the Manor were different from the ordinary run of mortals. The greater part of Lesser Sweeping belonged, and had always belonged, to the Stantons. They occupied an almost regal position — and the king could do no wrong.

MacDonald felt a little embarrassed as he awaited an answer to his ring at the front door.

'Supposing you're wrong, sir?' whispered Blane uneasily.

'We can only apologise,' said MacDonald. 'We're only doing our duty.'

They were shown into the library where Sir Robert was pacing restlessly up and down. He turned quickly as they came in.

'You have news?' he asked anxiously.

'No, sir,' said MacDonald. 'There is no further news of your brother . . . '

'What can have happened to him?' broke in Sir Robert. 'Have you searched everywhere? He may have been taken ill . . . '

'The fact is, sir,' said the superintendent, 'that we are under the impression that Mr. Richard Stanton is being . . . ' He found it difficult to make a direct accusation. 'Well, is being looked after by friends . . . '

'What do you mean — friends?' exclaimed Sir Robert. 'I don't know of anyone round here . . . '

'I'll not beat about the bush, sir,' said MacDonald bluntly. 'I'd like your permission to search this house.'

Sir Robert stared at him incredulously. Then his face turned a deep shade of purple.

'W — what the devil do you mean?' he cried, stammering slightly in his rage. 'Are you insinuating that I — that we — are — are concealing Richard *here* . . . '

'Aye, I am,' said MacDonald. 'I can

find no other explanation for his continued disappearance.'

'I — I have never been so insulted before in my life!' roared Sir Robert. 'By Jupiter, I've never heard such insolence . . . '

'I'll be willing to apologise if I'm wrong,' said the superintendent. 'Have we your permission to search the house, sir?'

Blane thought, in alarm, that Sir Robert was about to have a stroke.

'No, you have *not* my permission, and, what's more, you will not *get* my permission!' bellowed Sir Robert in a paroxysm of fury. 'How dare you come here and — and accuse me of — of — of . . . ' His voice died away in a spluttering search for words.

'I'm sorry you should take it this way, sir,' he interposed quietly. 'But, I should warn you that if you refuse to permit a search of this house to be made, I can easily obtain a warrant . . . '

'To blazes with your warrants!' cried Sir Robert. He snapped his fingers contemptuously. 'I don't care a fig for . . . '

'What's the matter, dear?' broke in a

woman's voice and Lady Stanton came in quickly. 'What are you annoyed about?'

'These — these men want to search the house,' said Sir Robert in a slightly quieter tone. 'They accuse me of — of harbouring Richard . . . '

'But how ridiculous,' interrupted Lady Stanton. 'Of course, we know nothing about Richard. Didn't you tell them so?'

'Tell 'em? I didn't tell 'em anything,' retorted Sir Robert. 'Except that I refused to allow them to search the house . . . '

'Why?' said Lady Stanton surprisingly. 'Why not let them search the house, if they want. We've nothing to hide.'

'It's the principle of the thing, my dear,' said her husband. 'These people think they can ride rough-shod over everybody . . . '

'That's not quite right, sir,' put in MacDonald. 'We've got our duty to do . . . '

'That's all right, superintendent,' said Lady Stanton graciously. 'We quite understand your position. My husband is naturally annoyed that you should suspect us of hiding Mr. Richard Stanton here, so please do whatever you wish. I only ask that you should be as quiet and as quick as you can.'

'Yes, yes,' grunted Sir Robert. 'You're quite right, Harriet. Sorry, I lost my temper.'

MacDonald and Blane searched the entire house, every nook and every cranny, but they found no trace of Richard Stanton. The superintendent apologised to both Sir Robert and Lady Stanton.

'I regret having troubled you,' he said as he took his leave. 'I'm sure you will understand that we cannot neglect anything that might lead to the discovery of this man.'

Sir Robert looked as though he might blow up again at hearing his brother referred to in this way, but he controlled himself.

'I hope you're satisfied,' he grunted.

But Superintendent MacDonald was far from satisfied. He was extremely worried. What the deuce *had* happened to Stanton? It kept running through his mind, like a musical refrain, as he drove back to Midchester.

The man must be *somewhere*. Where, where, where?

Nothing had come in when he reached his office. The widespread net was still out but there was no catch. Somehow or other, Stanton had succeeded in slipping through the mesh. But how he had done it was a mystery . . .

MacDonald sat racking his brains to find a solution, but without result. And then the afternoon brought with it a fresh problem which wiped all thought of the whereabouts of Richard Stanton from his mind.

Bluebeard posted the third key.

16

The news reached Superintendent Mac-
Donald by telephone just after three-thirty.
The postman who cleared the village box
had found a small parcel addressed to the
Reverend Colin Armitage at the vicarage
and had immediately notified the post
office according to instructions; the
post office, in turn, reported the matter to
MacDonald.

The superintendent drove over and
collected the parcel. There was not much
doubt as to its contents. It was a replica
of the other two parcels.

In less than an hour from the time he
had received the first intimation, Mac-
Donald was at the vicarage and discussing
it with the vicar.

'Well, it seems you were right, sir,' said
the superintendent, looking at the key
and the slip of paper that had accompanied it. 'I don't know how you guessed
that there'd be a third.'

'I thought it was more than likely,' said the vicar. 'This is exactly the same as the previous ones, you see.'

MacDonald nodded.

The key was not a Yale this time, like the one to the district nurse's house. It was a larger and older key. The message, in printed lettering on the slip of paper, ran:

'THIS IS BLUEBEARD'S THIRD KEY'

'Well, we're ahead of our friend Bluebeard this time, I imagine,' said the vicar. 'I wasn't expected to receive this until the first delivery in the morning. Therefore, I should say the murder is planned for tonight. We should be in time to prevent it . . . '

'Aye, sir,' said MacDonald, 'only you've forgotten an important item. We don't know *where* this key belongs . . . '

'I hadn't forgotten that most important point,' said the Reverend Colin Armitage. 'It's a difficulty that I foresaw . . . '

'It's going to be a pretty big one, sir,' said the superintendent. 'We can't go round trying to find a lock that this key will fit. If we do it'll come to the murderer's ears and he'll lie low. We don't want *that* . . . '

'No, now that we have a chance of catching him in the act so to speak, we must take advantage of it,' remarked the vicar, wrinkling his forehead. 'He has no knowledge that we have this key already in our possession and can go about his plans in a more or less leisurely fashion . . . '

'Which is a great deal more than we can do, sir,' said MacDonald. 'The time element with us is urgent. We know that a murder is going to be committed some time tonight, but we don't know who is going to be murdered or where the murder is to take place.'

'Both of which would be solved if we knew where this key belonged,' said the vicar. He picked it up and looked at it, holding it up to the light and turning it this way and that. 'I think,' he remarked, 'we can take it for granted that the house is not a new one. Not,' he added dubiously, 'that that helps very much.

216

There are not a great number of new houses in Lesser Sweeping.'

'But a considerable number of the type of house that this key would belong to, sir,' said the superintendent. 'It's a pretty tough puzzle.'

'It is indeed,' agreed the vicar, passing his hand over his thin hair. 'We cannot afford to make a mistake, you see. The result would be — unthinkable . . . '

If they made a mistake, thought the superintendent, somebody would be murdered that night — yes, unthinkable. They must be *sure*.

'I believe,' said the vicar suddenly, 'that I can be of more use in this particular case than you can, superintendent.' He looked at his watch. 'The time is now twenty minutes past four,' he went on. 'I shouldn't imagine that our friend Bluebeard would begin to put his — er — plan into execution until ten at the latest. It is not dark until nearly half-past. No, I think we can safely say ten as a safe limit. Meet me here at precisely half-past nine, bringing with you Inspector Blane — we may need his assistance. By then I hope to be in a position to tell you the address to which this belongs.'

'How are you going to do that, sir?' demanded MacDonald.

'You will have to leave that to me,' said the vicar. 'I must ask you, however, not to try and do anything yourself. You might completely spoil my idea if you do. And the fact that we have the key must be kept a close secret. You will promise that?'

'Well, sir,' said the superintendent, 'suppose you fail? What then?'

'I don't think I shall fail,' replied the vicar. 'But if I do, I assure you that any other method would have the same result. I ask you to trust me.'

'You were certainly right about this third key, sir,' said MacDonald, 'and you were right about the first one . . . ' He considered, rubbing gently at his chin. 'All right, sir,' he said. 'I'll agree. But for the Lord's sake let me know, if you can, sooner than nine-thirty. I shall be on tenterhooks . . . '

'I shan't be feeling so happy myself,' said the vicar with a faint smile. 'I'd willingly let you accompany me but that would ruin the whole thing. Now, I must ask you to leave me. I have a great deal to do — dear me, yes, indeed, a great deal to do . . . '

* * *

James Gregory Hemming strolled slowly through the woods. It was a lovely summer evening but he kept to the deepest parts of the wood where the trees grew thickest. It was not that he was afraid of being seen but he was a man who believed in taking precautions. His dark, rather shabby suit blended with the shadows under the trees and rendered him almost invisible at a short distance away. Not that there was anyone likely to be about here to see him.

Presently he sat down on a fallen branch and looked at his watch. He had plenty of time. It would not be dark for some time yet. He went over the items of his scheme, one by one. Everything had worked out perfectly so far. There wasn't very much more to do now, and he was glad. He hadn't liked what he had had to do, but it was essential and he had done it. He felt no compunction, not a tinge of remorse. He had seen men die in the hell of war — die horribly, some of them. He had almost died himself that day on the Normandy beaches. He remembered that inferno of flame and smoke and noise. The man next to him had had his face almost blown away by a shell, and just before he'd been hit in the leg, he'd thought of the idea of exchanging identities. Nobody would wonder seeing an orderly in the R.A.M.C. bending over a wounded man ... James Gregory Hemming had died on that beach — officially ... It had been clever. It had freed him of his debts and Dorothy ...

But she'd found him ...

He fingered the clipped moustache on his upper lip. Yes, she'd found him ... quite by accident too. An unlucky accident for her, as it turned out, although she had thought she was in clover ...

His mind, as he sat waiting on the fallen branch, switched from the past to the future. He would go abroad, some-where where there was sunshine, laughter and gaiety — where life was less ruled by civil servants, and rules and regulations. He'd always hated rules and regulations. Freedom! That was the thing that made life worth living. Absolute freedom.

The sun was slanting now outside the wood, long shadows creeping over the fields and meadows.

It would soon be time . . .

*   *   *

To Superintendent MacDonald, that evening was the longest he had ever spent in his life. The hands of the big office clock on the wall seemed to him to hardly move. He was relying entirely on Armitage. Would the vicar be successful? Would he be able to find out where the key belonged in time? Who had posted it? Richard Stanton, stealing out from some hiding place? That was impossible. Stanton was well known in Lesser Sweeping; he would have been recognised at once. But if it wasn't Stanton, then who *was* it?

The clock had barely moved since he looked at it before. If he hadn't been able to hear the steady ticking he would have thought that it must have stopped . . .

Supposing Armitage didn't succeed? Supposing that there was another murder committed that night? There must be something that could be done, if Armitage failed? MacDonald shook his head. There was nothing. How could they trace one key in time . . .

Inspector Blane came in. The superintendent had suggested that he should come back to Midchester with him and wait at the police station there in case there was any sudden news from the vicar.

'Anything yet?' asked the inspector.

'No, not yet. There hasn't been time . . . '

'How does the vicar expect to find out?' asked Blane.

'I've no idea,' answered MacDonald. 'I wish I had. He asked me to trust him, and I am . . . '

'He's a clever chap, is the vicar,' said Blane. 'If there wasn't a good chance, he wouldn't have said so . . . '

'He didn't,' said MacDonald shortly.

'He must think there is or he wouldn't have taken it on,' affirmed the loyal inspector. 'He must've got an idea . . . '

'He's full of 'em,' said MacDonald. 'He's got a theory about this case, but I don't know what it is.' He rubbed his eyes as though they hurt him. 'I only hope that it's the right one.'

'We just wait here until we hear from him?' asked the inspector.

'No,' answered the superintendent. 'If we don't hear anything in the meanwhile, we meet the vicar at half-past nine at the Vicarage.'

Inspector Blane looked at the clock.

'We've got three and a half hours to wait,' he said.

* * *

The Reverend Colin Armitage sat for nearly an hour at his desk after Superintendent MacDonald had left. He sat slumped back in his chair with his eyes fixed on the ceiling. They looked blank, like the eyes of a blind man, but behind them his mind was working busily.

He fully realised the risk he was taking. If he was wrong, it would be too late to rectify his error. But, on the other hand, there was nothing else to do. According to the way he had reasoned the matter out, the key should fit a certain lock. If it didn't, he was wrong. If it did . . . ?

The thing would soon be put to the test. At least, he would know definitely, one way or the other, before his appointment with MacDonald and Blane. Carefully, with the precision of mind that worked out the plots of 'Armitage Crane's' novels, the vicar went over the small details which had originally led him to his conclusion. They were very slight. It was largely a question of imagination, but he was sure that he was right. He'd *got* to be right. A human life depended on it.

He got up from behind the desk, walked over to the window and looked out at the sunlit garden. For a moment he remained there, and then, kneeling down at the big easy chair, he prayed that he might be given guidance.

Going out into the garden, he found his wife and daughter sitting under the tree on the lawn.

'I am going out,' he said. 'I shan't be

very long, I hope . . . '

'Where are you going, Daddy?' asked Merle.

'I am paying a visit to — er — one of my parishioners,' replied her father.

'Who?' asked Mrs. Armitage.

The vicar affected not to have heard her.

'Don't wait dinner for me, my dear,' he said. 'I — er — may be late . . . '

He wandered away down the path that led to the garage. Mrs. Armitage looked after him.

'I wonder who he is going to see?' she said.

Merle shook her head.

'I think there's something in the wind,' she answered.

'What a peculiar expression, dear,' said her mother. 'Where *do* you pick them up? What does it mean exactly?'

'That something's happening,' said Merle. 'Superintendent MacDonald was here this afternoon and he looked a bit excited. He was with Daddy for a long time . . . '

Mrs. Armitage turned a troubled face towards her.

'Oh, dear,' she said. 'I do hope your

father isn't going to get mixed up with any more trouble. All these keys and things. Really, it's not at all the right thing for a clergyman. Why doesn't he leave all that to the police?'

'He loves it,' said Merle. 'I can't see why a clergyman shouldn't help to find a murderer, if he can.'

Mrs. Armitage sighed.

'It's very disconcerting,' she said.

* * *

The hands of the clock in Superintendent MacDonald's office pointed to eight o'clock. Inspector Blane sat motionless on a hard chair against the wall, but MacDonald was pacing restlessly up and down the small room, fidgeting with the papers on the filing cabinet, stopping to stare out of the window, doing all kinds of things that showed the state of his nerves.

'Nothing yet,' he muttered.

Inspector Blane did not answer. There was, he felt, nothing to say.

The hands of the clock crept slowly round to the half-hour.

Still nothing.

At a quarter to nine, MacDonald went to the door.

'Come on,' he said. 'We'll go to the Vicarage . . . '

* * *

The Reverend Colin Armitage had not returned when they reached the Vicarage.

Merle admitted them and demanded to know what it was all about. But the superintendent merely replied that they had an appointment with the vicar, and left it at that. She wasn't satisfied in the least, but she didn't ask, and MacDonald didn't volunteer any further information.

It wasn't quite yet half-past nine. There was still five minutes to go when they heard the sound of the vicar's car approaching.

'Here he is,' said MacDonald. 'Now what's the verdict . . . ?'

The Reverend Colin Armitage came hastily through the French window of the study.

'Well, sir?' demanded the superintendent before he could speak.

'It is very well,' said the vicar. 'Dear me, yes. My theory is the right one . . . '

'You know where the key belongs, sir?' asked MacDonald eagerly.

'Yes, yes,' said the vicar. He shook his head. 'Dear me,' he said gravely, 'this is really a very shocking affair — terrible. We are dealing with a very calculating, cold-blooded person. I shall be very glad indeed when it's all over . . . '

Superintendent MacDonald controlled a desire to throw something at the vicar. As calmly as he could, he said:

'*Would* you be a little more explicit, sir?'

The Reverend Colin Armitage glanced at his watch.

'There is hardly time for explanations, superintendent,' he said. 'We cannot afford to arrive too late . . . '

'Where are we going?' said MacDonald, valiantly choking down his exasperation.

'We're going to prevent another murder,' said the Reverend Colin Armitage.

17

The sun had set in a blaze of gold and purple and red, and with its setting, the fingers of dusk began to smear out the lines of the landscape to a uniform grey which grew darker and darker until it merged into the darkness of night.

There was no moon, but the sky was clear and the stars sparkled like a million jewels against a deep blue velvet setting. It was a very still night, that hushed stillness that is only experienced in the depth of the country.

There was only one light in the dim bulk of the house to which the Reverend Colin Armitage had led Inspector Blane and Superintendent MacDonald, one light that shone faintly behind drawn curtains in a upper window.

From the concealment of a clump of laurels, they watched it.

'We shall have to act quickly when the time comes,' murmured the vicar.

MacDonald nodded. He hadn't yet recovered from the shock of what the vicar had told him. If it hadn't been for the evidence of the key he would never have believed it.

'I think it would, perhaps, be as well,' whispered the vicar, 'if Blane went round to the back and kept a lookout. It would be disastrous if — er — Bluebeard should get in without our knowing . . . '

The inspector nodded and slipped silently away.

'Which way do you think he'll come?' asked MacDonald.

'There's no reason why he shouldn't come to the front,' said the vicar. 'He cannot suspect that we know anything. So far as he is aware we have not yet received the key . . . '

'That's true,' agreed the superintendent.

'As soon as he enters the house, we shall follow. Luckily we have the key . . . '

'And then we grab him,' said Mac-Donald with satisfaction.

'We don't do any such thing,' said the vicar. 'Dear me, that would spoil every-thing. We must wait till the very last moment. Almost in the act, you see. Otherwise, there will be no real evidence of his intention . . . '

'I don't like it,' muttered the superintendent. 'It's risky.'

'It's the only way,' said the vicar firmly.

They had been speaking in whispers that were almost inaudible and now they lapsed into complete silence. In the stillness of the night around them, they could make out the tiny sounds of insects and small animals among the shrubs and flowers. The scent of the roses drifted in waves of perfume to their nostrils and reminded MacDonald of that other house where Sylvia Shand had been done to death. A moth flew into his face and startled him as he brushed it away. They had no idea how long they would have to wait — it might prove to be quite a long vigil.

The superintendent felt an unusual excitement mingled with elation. This cold-blooded killer was coming for his last kill, and they would be waiting to prevent it and punish him for what he had already done. The superintendent

thought of Hollings and Miss Cheeseman. He hadn't much sympathy for the
Shand woman, or to give her her right
name, Mrs. Hemming. She had asked for
all she'd got. But those other two were
different. Hollings had had a wife and a
little boy of seven; Miss Cheeseman had
led a useful life and would have gone on
leading one. That was the cruelty of it . . .

MacDonald had no use for the modern
sympathetic attitude towards criminals of
all kinds and especially murderers. The
kid glove methods now in practice had
brought on an increase in crime. What
was wanted was a return to the birch and
the cat. That 'ud put a stop to all these
young hooligans who thought it was brave
to attack young girls and elderly people.
That was the only thing they cared about
— physical pain. Sending them to prison
or to reform schools only made them
heroes among their friends. Anyhow, the
prisons and reform schools were not strict
enough. As for murderers . . .

All this hysterical nonsense about
hanging. They hadn't shown any mercy to
their victims, why should any mercy be

shown to them? Perhaps some of 'em *were* mental. Well, if they were, they were better out of the world. What was the good of locking 'em up for a few years and then letting 'em out to do it all over again?

MacDonald was always hearing a lot about progress but he didn't think the world *had* progressed. It was his opinion that it had definitely grown worse — or the people in it had. There were no standards anymore, that was the trouble. Nobody lived up to anything. It was all very well to make fun of the old days, but they'd had a rigid principle of life and if you stepped outside it you were an outcast. Now, you could do anything and nobody cared. It was all wrong. It was affecting the children and the teenagers. The result was to be seen in all these teddy boys. People blamed the war a lot more than was necessary. It wasn't so much the war as the general laxness in everything. Take marriage. Women gave up their husbands and their children these days, without a thought. They flitted from one man to another and nobody thought anything of it. In the old days they'd have been cast out by everybody. It was almost the same with friendship. What had happened to the real, deep friendship of that period? No, thought MacDonald, you couldn't call washing machines and refrigerators, and television, progress. It was the people who had to progress, not their surroundings. And the people hadn't. They were most of 'em selfish, cruel, and immoral . . . Perhaps that was a bit sweeping, but they weren't any better. 'I'm all right Jack', that was the motto of the present and the rising generation . . .

In the midst of his thoughts, Mac-Donald felt a slight pressure on his arm.

'I think I can hear him coming,' breathed the vicar softly in his ear.

The superintendent stiffened. He strained his ears but he could hear nothing. The vicar must have been mistaken . . . And then he did catch a faint sound. It was the sound of a lock clicking. But it wasn't the lock of the front door. That was directly in front of them and the sound had come from somewhere to their left.

But there was definitely someone about. They could hear other movement now, very quiet and stealthy, but quite audible. Almost holding his breath, MacDonald listened. A faint footfall became audible coming in their direction, and presently they could make out a dim shadow passing by the laurel bushes behind which they were concealed. It moved slowly up the steps to the front door. There was a pause and then the faintest of faint clicks.

'He's opened the door,' breathed the vicar.

They couldn't see anything, but they had to wait in order to make sure the night marauder had gone inside and shut the door. After a couple of minutes, they moved forward.

'You go and collect Blane,' said the Reverend Colin Armitage. 'I'll go and open the door.'

MacDonald nodded. He moved away round to the back of the house where Inspector Blane had posted himself, and the vicar went on to the front door. The overhanging porch made it very dark here and he hoped devoutly that he had left a long enough time elapse for the murderer to be well inside the house. It would not be pleasant if he were lurking somewhere in that patch of darkness . . .

The vicar felt a little creeping of the spine as he moved cautiously up the steps.

The door was shut.

He let his pent up breath escape slowly. So far, so good. Now, came the really risky moment. Very gently he inserted the key in the lock. And then he got a shock of surprise.

The key refused to turn! The intruder had put the catch up! The vicar uttered a most un-vicar-like expletive under his breath. This was serious. If they couldn't get into that house in time . . . ?

The figures of Inspector Blane and MacDonald came dimly into view at the foot of the steps. The vicar explained, hastily, what had happened.

'We'd better try the back,' whispered the superintendent. 'There'll be more chance of getting in there than round here.'

They hurried quickly round to the back of the house. There was a veranda here with French windows opening onto it.

'This should be the easiest,' muttered MacDonald, as he mounted the shallow steps that led up to the veranda. 'It'll make a bit of a noise, though.'

'We shall have to risk that,' said the vicar. 'We dare not risk not being in time.'

The superintendent was at one of the French windows trying the handle. It was fastened. They listened but they could hear nothing from inside the house. From where they stood everything was dark.

'Let's try the other window,' whispered the vicar, and he led the way along to it. He turned the handle softly, and the window opened!

Silently as shadows they passed through, one after the other, into the room beyond. There was a smell of flowers mingled with a faint and expensive perfume. This room was the drawing-room. Both windows opened onto the veranda and somebody had, carelessly, forgotten to fasten one of them. It was a piece of luck.

The door into the rest of the house was shut and going over to it, the superintendent carefully opened it. A faint light coming from somewhere above showed him a wide hall and the foot of a heavily carpeted staircase. The light came from an upper landing.

After making certain that there was no one in the lower hall, MacDonald and the other two came quietly out of the drawing-room and paused at the foot of the staircase. There was no sound from above.

The superintendent looked at the vicar and made a gesture toward the stairs. The vicar nodded, and they began cautiously to mount the wide treads. The thick carpet completely deadened all sound, but if anyone had looked over the landing rail at the top of the staircase, they would have been bound to be seen. The light from the shaded lamp above shone fully down upon them.

But, apparently nobody did, for they reached the landing without any sign of their presence being known.

It was a broad landing, almost square, and there were three doors opening from it. There was not a sound anywhere. They might have been the only occupants of the house. They dare not linger here. They couldn't fail to be seen, and there was no place to take cover. Where was the man they had followed into the house? In one of those rooms, the doors to which opened on the landing? But which?

It was the vicar who heard the first sound.

It came not as they had expected — from the floor they were on — but from below!

It was the sound of a light step crossing the hall.

There was only one thing they could do to avoid discovery if the owner of the step ascended the staircase. There was a further staircase from the landing leading upward, and they moved quickly over to it and almost ran up to the second landing. From here, they could look over into the well of the staircase to the hall below.

A man was beginning to ascend the stairs.

He must have been down there, in the back part of the house, when they had come in through that window in the drawing-room. If they had had to force the window, he must have heard them . . .

The man came on noiselessly. He was carrying something in one of his hands — something that dangled from his fingers . . .

MacDonlad's hand tightened on the rail over which he was leaning. This was *not* the man he had expected to see. This man had a moustache and dark hair . . .

He looked quickly at the vicar at his side, but Armitage was too intent on watching that figure with the dangling cord in its hand, coming nearer and nearer, to see him.

The man reached the landing and paused. He cast a quick glance round. Had he heard something? Surely he couldn't have become suspicious that he was being watched?

No, he ran the cord that he held through his fingers and moved towards the middle of the three doors. When he reached it he paused again, but only for a minute; then he gently turned the handle, opened the door, and went in.

'Now,' whispered the Reverend Colin Armitage.

He led the way swiftly and silently down the stairs, across the landing to the open door. MacDonald and Blane were close at his heels, and they peered into the room beyond the open door, holding their breaths.

There was a dim light burning on a bedside table, a shaded light, the light they had seen from outside. In the bed a woman lay asleep; and by the bed, motionless, stood the man with the cord in his hand. He stood watching the sleeper. Perhaps some instinct warned her of danger, for she stirred restlessly.

As though the movement was a signal, the man with the cord suddenly swooped, like a bird of prey upon its victim . . .

MacDonald and Blane almost leaped the distance between the door and the bed. Before the startled figure knew what was happening, they had gripped him by the arms, while the vicar switched on the light near the door.

As the room became flooded with light, the woman in the bed started up with a scream of terror. Her hands flew up to her throat . . .

'It's all right,' said the vicar soothingly. 'It's all right . . . '

The man between Blane and Mac-Donald was struggling to free himself, but his efforts were of no avail against their combined strength . . . The woman in the bed was gasping for breath, her large, frightened eyes staring . . .

'Who . . . what . . . ?' She tried to get the words out, but they were slurred and almost incoherent.

'Get him out of the room,' said the vicar to MacDonald under his breath, and with a nod the superintendent forced the struggling man to the door and out on to the landing.

'Stop struggling will you?' grunted Mac-Donald. 'Get a grip on his collar, Blane . . . '

As the inspector obeyed, his hand came into violent contact with the man's head as he jerked it upwards at the same moment. The dark wig he was wearing fell off, and MacDonald knew why he had not recognised him as he came up the staircase.

His face no longer vacuous, but distorted with fury, Ronald Payne glared at him . . .

18

The shock of that night brought on a severe heart attack, and it was only by a miracle and the constant attention of Doctor Mortimer, that Elizabeth Payne recovered.

'Better if she hadn't, in my opinion,' said Mortimer gruffly. 'She was devoted to that scoundrel, poor soul. She'll never recover from *that*.'

'A heartless and thoroughly callous man,' said the vicar, shaking his head. 'He has not one redeeming feature. That is unusual, you know . . . '

It was four days later. Superintendent MacDonald and Doctor Mortimer were seated in the vicar's study. James Gregory Hemming, alias Ronald Payne, had been charged and committed for trial at the next assizes. MacDonald had been working to gather all the facts together for the prosecution and had seen very little of the vicar. He had come over this morning in search of information and found the doctor already after the same thing.

'Aye,' said the superintendent. 'I hope he'll hang. The world will be a better place without him.'

'I'd like to get the facts of this business,' grunted Mortimer. 'Why did he do all this, eh?'

'For money,' said MacDonald.

'He had plenty,' said the doctor. 'She never stinted him for money. He hadn't a penny of his own, of course . . . '

'He wanted the lot,' said the superintendent, 'and he wanted freedom from a chronic invalid . . . '

'Yes, indeed,' put in the vicar. 'I am afraid that Elizabeth Payne was doomed from the time he married her. I think his original intention was — er — merely to assist nature. He would have arranged some form of severe shock that would have killed her . . . '

'But his real wife came into the picture and he had to do something about it,' said MacDonald. 'You see, he'd committed bigamy when he married Elizabeth Selby. His wife held that over his head to get

244

money out of him . . . '

'It was the original marriage certificate that she kept in that hiding place under the carpet which she showed to her friend — er — Plush,' said the vicar. 'I guessed it was something of the kind when you told me . . . '

'But why all this rigmarole of the keys?' demanded the doctor, frowning. 'Why do all that?'

'It was Richard Stanton who inspired that, I think,' said the vicar. 'I am of the opinion that Payne — I shall continue to call him that, although it wasn't his real name — I am of the opinion that Payne is what you call an opportunist. There was definitely something — er — peculiar about Richard Stanton. When he was planning out some safe means of — er — getting rid of his legal wife, it probably occurred to him that if it could be made to look like the work of a homicidal maniac, Richard Stanton might, very easily, be suspected. That was the reason for the murder of Hollings . . . '

'Do you mean to tell me,' exclaimed the doctor, 'that he deliberately killed that man in order to throw suspicion on Stanton?'

The vicar inclined his head.

'It seems incredible that a human being could do such a thing,' he said, 'but that was the reason. It wasn't, I don't think, part of the original plan. As I said just now, Payne is an opportunist. He took advantage of — er — anything that would forward his schemes. I imagine that he was out that afternoon, in the woods, when he saw Richard Stanton and the man who was obviously following him, and the idea came to him then. He probably also saw Michael Ferrall, and realised that he had seen Stanton and Hollings too. But, if he had been in the wood, Ferrall wouldn't have seen him. He waited until Ferrall had gone; my daughter was there as well and brought him back to tea, and the coast was clear. Payne armed himself with a heavy stone, came quietly up behind Hollings and hit him. When the man had fallen unconscious, Payne probably called to Richard Stanton. Whatever actually happened, he persuaded Stanton to come back. And he dealt with him in the same way . . . '

'He took an appalling risk,' said the doctor. 'Supposing he'd been seen?'

'Well,' said the vicar, 'he had a good explanation. Stanton had attacked Hollings. He had had to knock Stanton out because he was violent. It would have been believed, you know.'

'I should have believed it,' agreed the superintendent, shaking his head. 'I was convinced that Richard Stanton was the man we were after . . . '

'When he was quite sure that there was no one about, he strangled Hollings, and tied up Stanton,' continued the vicar, gazing dreamily into space as though he were witnessing the actual scene. 'It wasn't very far to the back of his own house, you know, and he had quite a lot of time before I found Hollings's body. I don't know how he managed to convey Stanton to that shed where we found him . . . '

'He seems to have gone to an unnecessary amount of trouble,' grunted Mortimer.

'No, no, not unnecessary,' said the vicar. 'It was quite clever, really. If, after Elizabeth Payne had been found strangled in her bed, Richard Stanton had also been found semi-conscious at the foot of the staircase, what would have been the general opinion?'

'H'm yes, I suppose you're right,' said the doctor. 'Cunning devil!'

'Even if he had stated that Payne had knocked him out and kept him a prisoner, who would have believed him?' said the vicar. 'And Payne was supposed to be away that day . . . '

'How did he post the key if he wasn't in the village?' asked the doctor.

MacDonald smiled.

'He *was* in the village, sir,' he said. 'He took the ten forty-five train to London from Midchester, but he only went as far as the first stop, Egglesfield. There, he changed into his disguise in the public convenience, and took the next train back to Midchester. From Midchester, he travelled by bus to Lesser Sweeping. After posting the parcel, he waited in the woods until it was time to complete the job. It was all very carefully planned . . . '

'Never should have thought the chap had sufficient brains,' said Mortimer. 'I

always looked on him as a nincom-
poop . . . '

'A great many people under-rated
Ronald Payne,' remarked the vicar. 'I'm
afraid I did at first. But, of course, that P.
G. Wodehouse character was part of his
stock-in-trade. It served him in very good
stead.' He shook his head sadly. 'Under-
neath was sheer wickedness — sheer
wickedness. How he could ever have
contemplated killing Elizabeth, who had
given him everything she possibly could,
and loved him sincerely, I cannot
understand . . . '

'She's paying the best counsel in the
country to appear for his defence, sir,'
said the superintendent. 'Can you beat
that?'

'Queer things, women,' said Mortimer.
'Never can tell what they'll do. Get hold
of a good fellow who does everything he
can for 'em, an' they treat him like dirt.
Get hold of a chap like Payne and they
practically fall down an' worship him.
Unpredictable.'

'Any counsel will, I think, find it
particularly difficult to break down the

evidence against Payne,' said the vicar, thoughtfully. 'Our own evidence, yours, Blane's, and mine, superintendent, will be fairly convincing. I don't envy the defence . . . '

'How did you work it all out, Armitage?' asked Doctor Mortimer curiously. 'Understand it was you who guessed the right man.'

'Guessed is only partly correct,' said the Reverend Colin Armitage. He took off his glasses, looked at them, and put them on again. 'You see, I — er — never quite accepted Payne at his — er — face value.' He shook his head. 'It always seemed to me that nobody could be *quite* so inane as he appeared to be. And then, of course, the type of — er — vacuous young man that he portrayed was — well, rather old-fashioned.'

'Phoney,' said Mortimer.

'Yes, though it is an expression I — er — dislike,' said the vicar. 'However, I don't want you to imagine that I thought there was anything *wrong* with him — not in the way he has turned. But I did wonder more than once why he took so much trouble to — er — play a part. My conclusion was that he found it paid. When he married Elizabeth Selby I thought that was the solution. She obviously adored the — er — helpless futility — if that is how you would describe it. It appealed to the maternal instinct inherent in all women, but particularly in women of her type. I thought very little more about it until after the — er — murder of Sylvia Shand.'

'I can't see how you linked that up with Payne,' said the doctor.

'Oh, I didn't,' said the vicar hastily. 'Not at first, that is. It wasn't until I heard that the Shand woman had been married and that her husband had been in the forces, that I began to put two and two together. You see,' he added apologetically, 'I am used to working things out in the manner of a plot. It was quite evident, at least to me, that Sylvia Shand had come to Lesser Sweeping because of someone who was already here. If she'd been hiding from anyone she would hardly have — er — drawn attention to herself by those weekend parties which became the talk of the village. Then again, although she only had five hundred pounds in her banking account when she came, she was living in a more expensive manner than such a sum justified. It seemed to me that it was a case of — er — blackmail. She knew something about somebody, living in the district, that they were paying her to keep silent about.' The vicar paused, and stroked his forehead.

'It is always very difficult to explain the actual processes of thought,' he went on, 'but I had got so far when I received the second key and we discovered the murder of Miss Cheeseman. The letter which she wrote to her sister was most illuminating. It now seemed clear, after Superintendent MacDonald told me what the sister had said, that the person we wanted was this missing husband. He had previously tried to strangle his wife — and that wife, from what Miss Cheeseman had told her sister, was Sylvia Shand. If it was the *husband* who had killed her, and that seemed to me certain because otherwise there was no point in the murder of Miss Cheeseman, then it was possible that the hold she had on him was just that — that he *was* her husband. That wouldn't produce a hold in itself without something to go with it — that he had married again. In other words — committed bigamy.'

'It seems pretty clear as you put it, sir,' agreed MacDonald. 'It didn't seem so clear at the time . . . '

'That was because you were occupied with the possibility of Richard Stanton and homicidal mania,' said the vicar, smiling. 'But I never thought that this business was the work of a homicidal maniac. It was far too cut-and-dried. As soon as the connecting link between Miss Cheeseman, Sylvia Shand, and the unknown husband came to light I was certain. That missing husband was somewhere in the district. He had killed his wife to silence her, he had killed the district nurse because he had recognised her and he was afraid that she would recognise him. But who could he be? Well, the person who obviously stuck out a mile, as they say, was Ronald Payne. He was a newcomer to the village, that is comparatively, and he had fairly recently married a very rich woman — ample reason for blackmail, when you think that a word from his real wife would have broken up the 'marriage' completely.'

'Pity she didn't say it,' grunted Mortimer.

'I was afraid,' said the vicar, ignoring the interruption. 'I was terribly afraid, because to logically complete the plan there might be another murder — Elizabeth Payne . . . '

'Then you knew when that third key arrived,' said the superintendent reproachfully, 'that it belonged to the Paynes' house?'

The vicar shook his head.

'I didn't,' he said. 'I suspected, but I wasn't certain. In my capacity as — er — vicar of the parish, I called that evening on Mrs. Payne. I discovered that her husband had gone to London to take some important documents to her solicitors. He had left on the ten forty-five from Midchester that morning. My heart sank. Were all my conclusions wrong? How could he have posted that parcel in Lesser Sweeping if he was in London? If I was wrong there was no time to rectify my error — there was another murder planned for that night and I had no idea *where*. It was not until I was on my way out that I was able to do what I had come there for — try the key I had in the lock of the front door. It fitted! I had been right!' In his excitement at reliving that moment, the vicar rose from his chair and began to pace up and down the room. 'You've no idea of the relief! I should never have forgiven myself if I'd been wrong, but now . . . Dear me,' he stopped and rubbed his forehead, 'I'm afraid I got quite carried away with — with my recapitulation . . . '

'Well, I congratulate you, sir,' said MacDonald heartily. 'I consider you worked it out very cleverly . . . '

'So do I,' put in Doctor Mortimer.

'How is Richard Stanton?' asked the vicar.

'He'll be ill for some time,' said Mortimer. 'On top of the blow he got from Payne, he was filled up with some form of barbiturate . . . '

'I hope Sir Robert will send him to a convalescent home of some kind,' said the vicar. 'By the way, I wish you'd have a word with Michael Ferrall. Do it tactfully. He's got it into his head that — er — the family taint might come out in his children . . . '

'Did he tell you that?' asked Mortimer.

'No, no, no,' said the vicar hastily. 'But I believe that it is so . . . '

'More deductions?' grunted Mortimer. 'Well, it's a lot of rubbish — poppycock! That young feller's as healthy as a bull — both physically and mentally. I'll tell him so . . . '

'Be tactful,' urged the vicar.

'Tact isn't my strong point,' said the doctor. 'Why are you so interested, eh?'

'My daughter wants to marry him,' said the Reverend Colin Armitage.

★ ★ ★

Mrs. Armitage looked across the breakfast table at her daughter and sighed. Her pleasant face wore an expression of half-humorous irritability.

'It really is too bad of your father, Merle,' she said. 'The coffee's cold and his bacon will be quite spoiled . . . '

The door opened and Linda came in with a jug of hot water.

'Did you tell the vicar that breakfast was ready, Linda?' asked Mrs. Armitage.

'I've told 'im twice,' said Linda.

'Go and tell him again, there's a good girl,' said Mrs. Armitage. Linda nodded and went out. 'It really is most annoying,' complained Mrs. Armitage. 'I *do* wish something could be done to make your father punctual for his meals.'

'You know what Daddy's like,' said Merle.

'Indeed I do, dear,' said her mother. 'It's a wonder to me that he hasn't starved to death long ago!'

'He's just started a new book,' said Merle. 'He'll be impossible for a week at least.'

'Yes, I suppose so,' sighed Mrs. Armitage.

The vicar opened the door and came in.

'What time is lunch?' he inquired, smiling benignly at them both.

'Really, Colin,' said Mrs. Armitage. 'You haven't had your breakfast yet.'

A look of surprise came into the vicar's face.

'I distinctly remember the kidneys on toast,' he said.

'That,' said Merle, 'was yesterday.'

'Dear me,' exclaimed her father, 'I was

quite certain that I had it this morning . . . '

'There's bacon and eggs this morning, Colin,' said Mrs. Armitage. 'You'd better sit down and have it now.'

'Yes, my dear, certainly,' replied the Reverend Colin Armitage. 'I cannot quite make up my mind whether to end chapter two with the finding of Throstle Wainwright impaled on the tree . . . Ah, yes, of course! Excuse me.' He turned and walked quickly to the door, bumping into the untidy Linda as she came in with the morning post.

'Good gracious, really, I'm extremely sorry,' said the vicar. 'What is that you have in your hand, Linda?'

'Two letters for Miss Merle and a small parcel for you,' said Linda. She thrust the letters and the parcel into the vicar's hand and went out.

'Now, I wonder what this can be,' murmured the Reverend Colin Armitage, peering through his glasses at the small packet in his hand.

Merle's face was pale as she stared at him.

'Daddy,' she cried. 'Don't open it!'

He blinked at her in astonishment.

'Why on earth not?' he asked.

'I — I'm sorry,' she said, flushing slightly. 'It was silly of me. I remembered — that other time . . . '

'This is nothing of that sort, my dear,' said the vicar. He ripped off the wrapping and disclosed a small cardboard box. In it lay a slim packet of printed cards.

'Invitation cards for your wedding,' said the Reverend Colin Armitage, smiling.

THE END

We do hope that you have enjoyed reading this large print book.

Did you know that all of our titles are available for purchase?

We publish a wide range of high quality large print books including:
Romances, Mysteries, Classics
General Fiction
Non Fiction and Westerns

Special interest titles available in large print are:
The Little Oxford Dictionary
Music Book, Song Book
Hymn Book, Service Book

Also available from us courtesy of Oxford University Press:
Young Readers' Dictionary
(large print edition)
Young Readers' Thesaurus
(large print edition)

For further information or a free brochure, please contact us at:
Ulverscroft Large Print Books Ltd.,
The Green, Bradgate Road, Anstey,
Leicester, LE7 7FU, England.
Tel: (00 44) **0116 236 4325**
Fax: (00 44) **0116 234 0205**

GUILTY AS CHARGED

Philip E. High

A self-confessed murderer recounts the events that led up to an apparently unprovoked attack; a gruesome murder scene holds nasty surprises for the investigating officers; a man makes what amounts to a deal with the devil — and pays the price; caught up in events beyond his control, a bit-part player in a wider drama has his guardian angel to thank for his survival . . . These, and other stories of the strange and unaccountable, make up this collection from author Philip E. High.

THE CLARRINGTON HERITAGE

Ardath Mayhar

When Marise Dering marries Ben Clarrington and moves into the old mansion where the rest of the Clarringtons live, she's ordered to keep out of the closed-off sections of the third floor — but is not told why. It is only later that she learns the sinister family secrets . . . but has she been told all of them? As the family members begin perishing in odd and horrifying circumstances, Marise must try to uncover all the secrets of the Clarrington heritage . . .

THE GLASS ARROW

Gerald Verner

West Dorling is a quiet, remote village. So what brings three men to live thereabouts at practically the same time? None of them seems to pursue any professional employment, yet they live in some style. When a local learns their secret and threatens blackmail, the three meet to discuss this threat. But on arrival, two of them find the other lying dead, shot through the heart by a glass arrow. Before long a second has died in the same manner. Who is the mysterious archer and why use *glass* arrows . . . ?

JIMMY LAVENDER
CHICAGO DETECTIVE

Vincent Starrett

Jimmy Lavender — Chicago Detective. The name conjures images of gangland murders, Al Capone and illegal bootleg whiskey, but Lavender has more in common with Sherlock Holmes. In some of his most baffling cases, Lavender comes up against such brain-twisters as a marble fountain statue that seemingly comes to life and walks by night; a fiancé who goes missing on the eve of his wedding; a missing sack of uncut diamonds; and murder, robbery, and sudden death on the high seas!